“I want to spend the night with you.”

“One night,” Rashid said, and she recognized it as a warning. “That’s all I can offer you.”

“Perfect,” Tora said with a smile because that was all she wanted. One night to forget her scheming, cheating cousin. “One night is all I want.” Tomorrow she could pick up the shattered pieces of her promises and work out where she went from there.

His eyes glinted in the street lighting, a flash of victory that came with a spark of heat, and he reached out his fingers to push a wayward tendril of her hair behind her ear. It made her skin tingle. “My name is Rashid.”

“Tora,” she said, even as she trembled under his touch.

He took her hand and brought it to his mouth, pressing it to his lips. “Come, Tora,” he said.

Desert Brothers

Bound by duty, undone by passion!

These sheikhs may not be brothers by blood, but they are united by the code of the desert.

Their power and determination is legendary and unchallenged—until unexpected encounters with women strong enough to equal them threaten their self-control...

Read the two concluding stories in Trish Morey's exciting quartet of searing passion and sizzling drama!

Captive of Kadar
May 2015

Shackled to the Sheikh
November 2015

Trish Morey

Shackled to the Sheikh

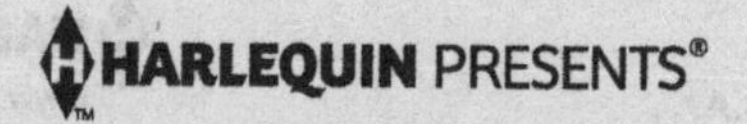

Recycling programs
for this product may
not exist in your area.

ISBN-13: 978-0-373-13866-1

Shackled to the Sheikh

First North American Publication 2015

This edition published by arrangement with Harlequin Books S.A.

For questions and comments about the quality of this book, please contact us at CustomerService@Harlequin.com.

Printed in U.S.A.

Trish Morey always fancied herself a writer—so why she became a chartered accountant is anyone's guess! But once she'd found her true calling there was no turning back. Mother of four budding heroines and wife to one true-life hero, Trish lives in an idyllic region of South Australia. Is it any wonder she believes in happy-ever-afters? Find her at trishmorey.com or facebook.com/trish.morey.

Books by Trish Morey

Harlequin Presents

A Price Worth Paying?
Bartering Her Innocence
The Heir from Nowhere
His Prisoner in Paradise
His Mistress for a Million

The Chatsfield

Tycoon's Temptation

Desert Brothers

Duty and the Beast
The Sheikh's Last Gamble
Captive of Kadar

Bound by His Ring

Secrets of Castillo Del Arco

21st Century Bosses

Fiancée for One Night

Dark-Hearted Desert Men

Forbidden: The Sheikh's Virgin

Visit the Author Profile page
at Harlequin.com for more titles.

To my amazing readers,
With grateful thanks and wishing you love always,
Trish

CHAPTER ONE

RASHID AL KHARIM was done with pacing.

He needed something stronger.

He needed to lose himself. To dull the pain of each and every one of today's revelations, if only for a few precious hours.

To forget about a father who hadn't died thirty years back as he'd always believed, but a scant four weeks ago.

And to forget about a tiny child—a sister—who apparently was now his responsibility…

His head full of anger and torment, he let the door of his Sydney hotel suite slam hard behind him as he strode towards the lifts, stabbing the call button with intent, because he knew exactly what he needed right now.

A woman.

CHAPTER TWO

GOD, SHE HATED dingy bars. Outside this one had looked like an escape from her anger and despair, but inside it was dark and noisy and there were far too many leering men who looked way too old to be hanging out in a place where the average age of women was probably somewhere around nineteen. Tora upped the demographic just by being there, she figured, not to mention lowered the average heel height by a matter of inches, but it didn't stop the old guys leering at her just the same.

But the bar was only a few steps from her cousin's office and after an hour remonstrating fruitlessly with him, an hour where nothing—neither her arguments nor her tears—had made a shred of difference, she'd needed to go somewhere where she could drink something strong and fume a while.

One of the old guys across the bar winked at her. Ugh!

She crossed her legs and pulled her skirt down as she ordered another cocktail.

God, she hated bars.

But right now she hated her financial adviser cousin more.

Financial adviser cheating scumbag of a cousin, she revised as she waited for her drink, wondering how long it would be before the damned alcohol was going to kick in so she might stop feeling so angry.

She really needed to forget about the curl of her cousin's lips when she'd refused to be put off any longer with his excuses and insisted he tell her when she'd be able to access the money she'd been due from her parents' estate.

She needed to forget the pitying look in his cold eyes when he'd finally stopped beating about the bush and told her that it was gone, and that the release she'd signed thinking it was the last formality before receiving a pay-out had actually been a release signing the money over to him—only now there would be no pay-out because he'd 'invested' it all on her behalf, only the investment had turned sour and there was nothing left. Nothing at all left of the two hundred and fifty thousand dollars she'd been counting on. Nothing at all left of the money she'd promised to loan to Sally and Steve.

'You should have read the small print,' he'd said ever so smugly, and she'd never had violent tendencies before but right then she'd really fancied doing someone some serious bodily damage.

'Blood is thicker than water,' her parents had insisted, when they'd chosen their nephew Matthew over the financial planner she'd nominated, the father of a woman she'd known and trusted since primary school. And Tora had shrugged and conceded it was their choice, even if her cousin had been the kind of person who'd rubbed her up the wrong way all her life and never someone she'd choose as a friend, let alone her financial adviser.

For damned fine reason, as it had turned out.

Her cocktail arrived and her fingers curled around the stem of the glass as she studied it.

Now she had to work out a way to tell Sally she wouldn't be getting the promised funds, after assuring her—because Matt had promised—that settlement was all on track and that the funds would be coming any day. She felt ill just thinking about it. They'd been counting on her—counting on this money. She shook her head. She would have to find another way, go back to the banks and try again. *Try harder.*

She lifted the glass to her lips and it was all she could do not to swallow the drink down in a rush, wanting the buzz, hoping for the oblivion it promised.

'Hi there, sweet lips. You look like you needed that. Fancy another?'

She blinked against a sudden flash of strobe

and opened her eyes to see one of the leery old guys shouldering his way alongside her at the bar, this one with a decent paunch and a skinny ponytail and with a possessive arm curling its way around the back of her seat. Across the bar his friends were watching and grinning as if this was some kind of spectator sport, and their ponytailed friend might have been right about her needing another drink but not if it meant waking up next to this guy. Suddenly getting a taxi home where there was a half-empty bottle of Riesling in the fridge seemed a far better option than staying here and seeking oblivion amongst this lot. She reached for her bag.

The bar was too noisy. Too dark.

Almost immediately Rashid regretted the impulse that had seen him climb down the stairs to the noisy bar in the basement of the building alongside his hotel.

Because the questions in his mind were still buzzing, and as his eyes skated over a dance floor filled with young women wearing more make-up than clothes he wasn't convinced he was going to find the relief he needed here.

He ground his teeth together, the fingers that had been bound so tightly today already aching to curl once more into fists.

He was wasting his time here. He turned to

leave, and that was when he saw the woman sitting by herself at the bar. His eyes narrowed. She was attractive, he guessed, under that bookish exterior, and she sure looked out of place here, standing out in her short-sleeved shirt in a sea of otherwise bare flesh. Too buttoned up with her brown hair pulled back into a tight bun. A glass of milk in a wine bar wouldn't have looked more out of place.

But at least she looked as if she was past puberty. At least she looked like a woman.

He watched her down half her cocktail and scowl into the glass, but not as if she was morose, more as if she was angry. So she was as unimpressed with the world as he was? Perfect. The last thing he needed was someone with stars in their eyes. Maybe they could be angry at the world together.

He was already edging his way through the crowd when a man sidled up to her and slipped his arm around her back.

Rashid suppressed a growl and turned away. He might be angry, but he wasn't about to fight over a woman.

'I'm not actually looking for company,' Tora said to her persistent would-be friend. Sure, someone sympathetic to get the whole sorry cheating-cousin saga off her chest might be therapeutic.

Someone to lend her a shoulder and rub her back and say it would all be okay might be nice, but she hadn't come here looking for that and she wasn't about to consider any offers, not if the sympathetic shoulder came packaged like this one.

'Just when we were getting on so well, too,' he said, moving his bulk sideways when he saw her picking up her clutch to block her from getting up from her stool.

'I hadn't noticed,' she said, mentally adding another hate to her growing list—leery men in bars who imagined they were God's gift to women, although, to be honest, that one had always been right up there with seedy bars. 'And now if you wouldn't mind getting out of my way?'

'Come on,' he said, curling his arm closer around her back, and breathing beer fumes all over her. 'What's your rush?'

It was when she turned her head to escape the fumes that she saw him. He moved like a shadow in the dark basement, only the burst of coloured lights betraying his movements in the glint of blue-black hair and the whites of his eyes under the lights. He was tall and looked as if he was searching for someone or something, his eyes scanning the room, and, while heads turned in his wake, so far nobody seemed to be laying claim to him.

Surprising, given the way he couldn't help but be noticed if someone was waiting for him.

Not to mention convenient.

'How's about I get you another drink?' the man offered, slurring his words. 'I'm real friendly.'

Yeah, she thought, if only he were sober and could speak clearly and looked a little more like the man who'd just walked in, she might even be interested.

'I'm meeting someone,' she lied, pushing off her stool but making sure it was her shoulder that brushed past his stomach and not her breasts. Her feet hit the ground and even on her sensible heels, she wobbled. Whoa! Maybe those cocktails weren't such a total loss after all.

'He stood you up, eh?' said the man, still refusing to give up on his quarry. Still refusing to believe her. 'Lucky I'm here to rescue you from sitting on the shelf all night.'

'No,' she said, in case Mr Beer Breath decided to argue the point, 'he just walked in,' and she squeezed her way past him determined to prove it.

Half-heartedly Rashid scanned the room one last time, already knowing that he was wasting his time in this place. He turned to leave—he would find no oblivion here—when someone grabbed his arm.

'At last,' he heard a woman say above the music. 'You're late.'

He was about to say she was mistaken and shrug her off, when her other arm encircled his neck and she drew herself closer. 'Work with me on this,' she said as she pulled his head down to hers.

It was the woman at the bar—that was his first surprise—and the only thing that prevented him from pushing her away. The fact Ms Bookish had turned into Ms Bold and Brazen was the second. But she'd saved the best for last, because her kiss was the biggest and the best surprise of all. She tried to get away after a moment but her lips were soft, her breath was warm, and she tasted of fruit and alcohol, summer and citrus, all over warm, lush woman, and she wasn't going anywhere just yet. He ran his arm down her back, from her shoulder to the sweet curve of her behind, his fingers curling as they squeezed, and she arched into him as she gasped in his mouth.

Yes. This was what he needed.

This was what he'd come looking for.

Maybe coming here tonight hadn't been such a bad idea after all.

'Let's go,' she said, purposefully, if a little shakily, as she pulled away, her eyes shot with surprise as she looked from him over her shoulder to where she'd been sitting. He followed her gaze and saw the men lined up at the bar watching her, saw the slap to the back in consolation to the man who'd been talking to her, and he half wondered what the man had said to her that she seemed so shaken now. Not that Rashid really cared, as he wrapped an arm around her shoulders and cut through the crowd heading for the stairs and the exit, given he'd ended up exactly where he'd wanted.

Tora's heart was thumping so loud, she was sure it was only the thump-thump of the music in the bar that was drowning it out. She must be more affected by the alcohol than she'd realised.

Why else would she have walked up to a complete stranger and kissed him?

Though it wasn't just the alcohol fuelling her bravado, she knew. It was the anger, first for her cheating cousin, secondly for that meat market of a nightclub and a creep of a man who imagined there was any way in the world she'd want to spend even a moment with his beery self. And it hadn't been enough simply to walk away—she'd been wanting to show him she wasn't some sad lonely woman who'd be flattered to have his attention. Well, she'd sure shown him well and good.

But a peck on the lips in greeting was all she'd intended. A signal to the men watching that she wasn't alone. She hadn't expected that man to be so willing to join in her game. Nor had she expected to be sideswiped by a stranger's taste and touch in the process, leaving her dazed and confused. And the way her skin tingled and sparked when their bodies brushed as they walked side by side—well, that was interesting, too.

She willed the itching fingers on the hand she'd wrapped around his waist to be still, but, God, it wasn't easy, not when he felt so hard, so lean. Oh, wow… She needed to get outside and let the night air cool her heated skin. She needed the oxygen so she could think straight. She needed to say thank you to this stranger and get herself a taxi and go home, before she did anything else crazy tonight.

Because tonight was shaping up to be all kinds of crazy and the way this man felt, she wasn't sure she could trust herself.

And then they were out on the street and the nightclub door closed behind them and she never got a chance to say thank you because he was pulling her into the shadows of a nearby doorway and kissing her all over again and she was letting him and suddenly it wasn't the alcohol or her anger that was affecting her—it was one hundred per cent him.

Madness, she thought as his masterful lips coaxed open hers. She should put a stop to this, she thought as his tongue danced with hers. She didn't do things like this. They might be in the shadows but they were on a public street after all. What if Matt saw her on his way home?

And then her anger kicked in and she thought, damn Matt, why would she care what he thought? Let him see. And she pressed herself closer.

A moment later she stopped caring about anything but for the hot mouth trailing kisses up her throat to her mouth, his hands holding her tight to him so they were joined from their knees to their lips and every place in between felt like an erogenous zone.

'Spend the night with me,' he whispered, drawing back to whisper against her ear, his breath fanning her hair, fanning the growing flames inside her in the process, and she almost found herself wishing he'd said nothing but carted her off to his cave so she didn't have to think about being responsible. Crazy. She didn't meet strangers in bars and spend the night with them.

'I don't even know your name.' Her words were breathless, but it was the best she could manage when her mind was shell-shocked and every other part of her body was busy screaming *yes*.

'Does it matter?'

Right now? God, he had a point. He could tell her his name was Jack the Ripper and she'd have trouble caring. But still…

'I should go home,' she managed to say, trying to remember the good girl she always figured she was and the plan she'd had—something about a taxi and a bottle of Riesling in the fridge and a cheating cousin she wanted to forget about—but she was having trouble remembering the details and wasn't that a revelation?

Wasn't that what tonight was supposed to be all about—forgetting?

He pulled away, letting her go even though the distance between them was scant inches. Even now her body swayed into the vacuum where his had so recently been. 'Is that what you want? To go home?'

She saw the tightness in his shadowed features as if it was physically hurting him to hold himself back, she felt the heat rising from his strong body and she knew what it must be costing him to leave her to decide when the power in his strong limbs told her that he was powerful enough to take whatever he wanted. The concept was strangely thrilling. The perfect stranger. Powerful, potentially dangerous, but giving her the choice.

A choice never so starkly laid out in her mind.

A choice between being responsible and playing it safe and going home and sitting stewing about what she'd missed, or being reckless for once in her life and taking what was on offer—one night with a man whose touch promised to make her forget all the things she'd wanted to forget. One night with a stranger. Her cousin would be horrified, and right now wasn't that good enough reason in itself?

Besides, all her life she'd played it safe, and where had that got her? Nowhere. She'd done nothing wrong and yet she'd lost more today than she'd ever thought possible.

Tonight was no night to play it safe.

'No,' she said, her tongue tasting an unfamiliar boldness on her lips. 'I want to spend the night with you.'

'One night,' he said, and she recognised it as a warning. 'That's all I can offer you.'

'Perfect,' she said with a smile because that was all she wanted. 'One night is all I want.' Tomorrow she could pick up the shattered pieces of her promises and work out where she went from there.

His eyes glinted in the street lighting, a flash of victory that came with a spark of heat, and he reached out his fingers to push a wayward tendril of her hair behind her ear, making her skin tingle. 'My name is Rashid.'

'Tora,' she said, even as she trembled under his touch.

He took her hand and brought it to his mouth, pressing it to his lips. 'Come, Tora,' he said.

CHAPTER THREE

NICE, SHE REGISTERED vaguely as he swept her through the marble-floored lobby of one of the oldest and classiest hotels in Sydney. Very nice. People dreamed of spending a night at The Velatte—ordinary people, that was. Clearly the man at her side was no ordinary person. But then, she already knew that. No ordinary person had ever set her pulse racing just by his presence. No average garden-variety man had ever set fires under her skin merely with his touch.

And now it was anticipation of a night with this far from ordinary man making the blood spin around her veins and her knees feel weak.

The lift whisked them to a high floor, his arm wound tightly around her, another couple in the lift the only thing that kept him from pulling her into his kiss, if the heated look in his dark eyes she caught in their reflection in the mirrored lift walls was any indication—mirrored panels that also gave her the chance to steal a closer look at the man she'd agreed to spend the night with. The flash of strobe in the darkened bar had shown her a face of all straight lines and planes—the dark slash of brows, the sharp blade of his nose, the angles of his jaw—but now she could see the softer lines of his mouth and the fullness of his bottom lip and the curve of flesh over high cheekbones. The combination worked.

It was then she realised that his eyes weren't black but the deepest, deepest blue, like the surface of the bottomless ocean on a perfectly calm day.

He was beautiful, way too beautiful to be by himself, and the good girl in her wondered why he was, while the bad girl in her—the newly found bad girl who drank cocktails in basement bars and threw herself at random men on a whim—rejoiced. Because right now she was the one here in this lift with him.

He opened the door to his room that turned out to be a suite because it was a sitting room they entered, decorated in modern classics in grey and cream and illuminated with standing lamps, lending the room a subtle golden glow. Oh, no, this man was definitely not ordinary. He was either loaded, or his employer's accountant was going to have a heart attack when the expense-account bill came in.

'It's huge,' she said, overwhelmed, wondering just who this man she'd met in a nightclub and with whom she'd agreed to a night with actually was.

'I got an upgrade,' he said dismissively, as if that explained a suite fit for a king, as he headed towards a phone. 'Something to drink?'

Her mouth was dry but only because every drop of moisture in her body had been busy heading south ever since he'd asked her to spend the night. 'Anything,' she said, and he ordered champagne for two and put the receiver down, the fingers of one hand already unbuttoning his shirt.

'The bedroom's through here,' he said as he led the way into a room with furniture in both gloss white and dark timber, with white louvre glass doors opening onto a terrace beyond. A super-king-sized bed with a plump quilted headrest and snowy white bed linen held pride of place against the opposite wall.

'So,' he said as he reefed off his shirt and tossed it onto a chair in the corner, exposing a chest that wouldn't have looked out of place on her annual firefighters' fundraising calendar. 'Shower first?'

She stood transfixed, drinking in his masculine perfection, the sheer poetry of tightly packed muscle under skin, until his hands moved to his belt, and with a jolt she realised she should be doing something, too, not standing around ogling him and waiting to be seduced.

This wasn't a seduction after all. Clearly he'd done his seducing in getting her here. This was more like getting down to business.

'Oh, right,' she said, her tummy a mass of flutters, the bad girl inside her overruled by the good girl who was suddenly aware of how far out of her league she was, and not just because this man came with serious money. Here he was, shedding clothes and shoes in a lighted room more easily than an autumn tree shed its leaves in the wind and no doubt expecting her to do likewise. She slid off her shoes, her fingers playing at her buttons as she remembered what she'd put on this morning, wishing she'd worn something a bit more exciting under her boring black skirt and shirt than her even more boring underwear. Not that she had a seduction collection, exactly, but she might have managed to wear something that at least smacked of lace.

She swallowed as she pulled the shirt free from the waistband of her skirt and eased it over her shoulders, feeling more self-conscious by the second as she stood there in her department-store skirt and regulation bra. 'I didn't dress for…'

He looked at her, a frown tugging at his brows, as he shrugged off his trousers, revealing denim-coloured elastic fitted boxers that fitted his hard-packed body so well, there were no bulges anywhere—except where there should be.

*Oh, my...*she thought, her stomach flipping over, her mouth Sahara dry, and she wondered how long the champagne would take to arrive.

She didn't need the alcohol particularly, but her mouth sure could do with the lubrication.

'I'm not interested in your underwear,' he said as he padded on bare feet towards her, his steps purposeful rather than rushed. He lifted her chin with the tips of his fingers and pressed his lips lightly to hers while his other hand eased the tie from her hair, making her scalp tingle, pulling it free so that her hair tumbled heavily over her shoulders. His fingers skimmed down her throat and to her shoulder, found the strap of her bra and curled a fingertip beneath, before slipping it away down her arm. He pushed the hair back and dipped his head and pressed his lips to her bare shoulder and breath hissed through her teeth. 'I'm interested in what lies beneath.'

She shuddered on a sigh, her breasts achingly tight, as she felt his clever fingers at her back as he slid her bra away. And then her skirt was riding low and lower over her thighs before she realised he'd even unzipped it. 'Very interested,' he said, standing back to take her in, dark storm clouds scudding over the deep ocean blue of his eyes. He touched the pads of his thumbs to her bolt-like nipples and twin spears of sensation shot down deep into her belly, triggering an aching pulse between her thighs. Her groan of need was out before she could haul it back, but he didn't seem to mind as he sucked her into a deep kiss that amplified the sensations.

'What happened to the brazen woman who accosted me in a bar?'

She was a fraud. Tora swallowed. 'She was angry. She was proving a point.'

'Is she still angry?'

'Yes, but now she just wants to forget why.'

'Oh,' he said, his eyes gleaming as he swung her into his arms and headed for the shower. 'I can make you forget.'

Her stranger was true to his words. Granted, he had steam, a rainforest shower head and slippery gel on his side, but his clever hands and mouth had a way of making her forget everything besides being naked with a man she wanted to bed her with a compulsion and an urgency she'd never felt before—an urgency he didn't seem to mirror.

When he'd turned on the taps and shucked off his underwear, she'd gasped at his size, not with fear, but with anticipation. She wasn't a virgin. She knew how things worked and what generally happened and, if she was totally honest, she'd always wondered what it would be like to make love with a man so well equipped. But then he'd hooked his fingers into the sides of her underwear and pushed them down and she'd imagined that a minute or two of foreplay in the form of soaping each other's skin, and they'd be making love right here in the shower.

Apparently he wasn't in such a rush.

He kissed her again, long and deep, as she clung to his shoulders, while the torrent rained down upon them, his slippery hands in her wet hair, down her throat to cup her breasts before sliding down her sides, the touch of his long fingers relaying the dip of her waist in a way she'd never felt or seen so clearly in her mind's eye before. Every curve his fingers seemed to find, every jut of bone explored on their seemingly leisurely but purposeful way south. It almost felt as if his fingers were mapping her terrain.

She gasped again, into his seeking mouth this time, when one hand cupped her mound. She felt his lips smile around hers before his mouth dipped to her throat, to kiss her shoulder and then worship her breasts on his way down to kneeling before her, his lips traversing her belly, his fingers deep between her thighs and the pulsing flesh that lay within.

Oh, God. She shuddered as he parted her legs, turning her face up into the spray as his fingers opened her to him. Exposed her to him. She thought she knew about sex. She'd thought this would be over in a minute. But she might just as well have known nothing. She felt like a virgin all over again.

She knew nothing at all, but…

Pleasure.

It came upon her in waves as his tongue lapped at her very core, teasing her beyond existence, beyond reason, as all she knew was sensation.

His tongue. The steam. The water cascading over her and his fingers teasing, circling her aching centre.

Right now there was nothing but sensation, and the inexorable build to a place a man had never taken her. A place she'd never believed it possible for a man to take her unassisted. This man was taking her all the way.

She felt his fingers stray closer until they edged inside her. She felt the tug of his mouth on her screaming nub of nerve endings and she felt the surge coming. She bit her lip to stop from crying out but there was no stopping the wave that washed over her and the cry that came all the same as her body broke around him.

He supported her before her knees could give way and she fell, and she felt him there, at her core.

Yes, she thought, because even on her way down from the highs he'd taken her to she still wanted this—wanted him deep inside her—more than anything.

But then, just as she thought she had him, just

as her muscles worked to urge him in, he pulled away on a curse and slammed open the shower door.

She blinked as he pulled a towel from a rack and wrapped it around her, swinging her into his arms.

'What's wrong?' she said, still trembling after her high and back to the virgin she wasn't, fearful she'd done something wrong.

'Nothing,' he said as he deposited her in the centre of the big wide bed before pulling out a drawer, 'that this won't fix.'

He tore the top from the foil packet and rolled the condom down on him and suddenly it made sense and she was glad one of them was still thinking.

'Now,' he said, his face grim as he positioned himself between her legs, 'where were we?'

And the virgin inside her turned wanton as she wrapped her hand around his bucking length and felt his power and his need within her fingers, and placed him at her core. 'Right here.'

His eyes flared with heat as he growled with approval, and her heart skipped a beat as he took her hands and pinned them each side of her head, their fingers intertwined, and then with one long thrust he was inside her and sparks went off behind her eyes.

It was sex, she had to remind herself, just sex,

because in that moment it had seemed that the world as she knew it revolved around that moment and that moment only.

He leaned down and kissed her then, so sweetly and reverently that she wondered if he'd felt it, too, this tiny spark of connection that went beyond physical, before he let go her hands and raised himself higher and slowly withdrew. She almost whimpered at the loss, wanting to hold him inside and keep him there, but then he was back, lunging deeper if that were possible, the slide and slap of flesh against flesh bringing with it that tidal flow of sensation, in and out and building each time until their bodies were slick with sweat. There was nowhere left to go, nowhere left to hide, and the next wave surge crashed over her and washed her away.

She clung to him as he went with her, tossed helplessly in the foaming surf of her undoing, gasping for air, not knowing which way was up.

He pressed his lips to her forehead before he slumped beside her. 'Thank you,' she heard him say between his ragged breaths, and she wondered if he could read her mind, for they were the exact same words she wanted to tell him.

He watched her sleep in the yellow-grey light, watched the slow rise of her chest and listened to the soft sigh as she exhaled, all the time wondering at a woman who had turned up exactly when he'd needed her. A woman who had made him forget the shocks of today so well that he'd almost forgotten to use protection.

When had that ever happened before?

Never, that was when.

He shook his head. He was more affected by today's revelations than he'd realised if he could forget something so absolutely fundamental. There could be no other reason for it. Other than the way she'd come apart so furiously that he hadn't wanted to wait, he'd wanted to follow her right then and there.

Propped up on his elbow, he lay alongside her, watching her eyelids flutter from time to time. Her hair splayed wild around her head and against the pillow. Tangled. Elemental. He touched a finger to one of the coils, felt the silk and steel within the shafts of hair and congratulated himself for walking down the stairs into that basement bar.

One night with a stranger had never been so desperately needed and so satisfying.

Almost.

He leaned over, pressed his lips to hers. Her eyelids fluttered open and momentary surprise gave way to a tentative smile. 'Oh, hi,' she said as her smile turned wary. 'Is it time for me to go?'

'No way,' he said as he pulled her into his arms. 'You're not going anywhere just yet.'

CHAPTER FOUR

IT WAS STILL dark when her phone buzzed, only dull yellow street light filtering up from the street far below sneaking between the gaps in the curtains. Disoriented and aching in unfamiliar places, Tora took a while to work out where she was let alone manage to stumble from the bed and find where she'd left her bag. Groggily she snatched up her mobile and stole a glance over her shoulder. Behind her Rashid lay sprawled on his front, legs and arms askew as he slept. He looked magnificent, like a slumbering god, somehow even managing to make a super-king-sized bed look small.

'Yes,' she whispered, and listened while Sally apologised for calling her on her day off, but it was an emergency and could she come in?

She closed her weary eyes and put a hand to her head, pushing back her hair. How much sleep had she had? Not a lot. Not a good way to go to work, especially not when she had news to tell her friend—bad news—and she'd really wanted more time before breaking it. 'Are you sure there's nobody else?'

But she already knew the answer to that or Sally wouldn't have been calling on the first day off she'd had for two weeks. 'One more thing,' Sally said, once she'd told her she'd be there in an hour. 'Pack a bag and bring your passport. Looks like you might need them.'

'Where am I going?'

'I'm not sure exactly. I'll fill you in on what I do know when you get here.'

Tora slipped her phone away and glanced once more at the man she'd left sleeping on the bed, the man who'd blown her world apart and put it back together again more times than she would have believed possible in just one night. She shouldn't be sorry there wouldn't be one more time, she really shouldn't. No, no regrets. It was a one-night deal and now that night was over. She gathered up her discarded shirt and skirt and abandoned underwear and dressed silently in the bathroom.

Leaving this way was better for both of them. At least this way there was no chance of an awkward goodbye scene. No chance of anyone expecting too much or appearing hopeful or needy.

He seemed like the kind of man who'd be relieved she wasn't going to hang around and argue the point.

She picked up her shoes and spared one last glance towards the bed.

One night with a stranger.

But what a night.

He'd done what he'd promised to do. He'd blotted out the pain and the anger of her cousin's betrayal. He'd taken her from feeling shell-shocked and numb with grief and for a few magical hours he'd transported her away from her hurt and despair to a world filled with unimaginable pleasure.

He'd made her forget.

She let the door snick behind her.

It was going to be a hell of a lot harder to forget him.

He woke with a heavy head from too little sleep and with a dark mood brewing yet still he reached for her. There were things he had to do today, facts he had to face from which there was no escaping—headaches, each and every one of them—but the lawyer and the vizier and the headaches could wait. There was something he wanted more right now in this drowsy waking time before he had to let the cold, hard light of day hit him, as he knew it soon would. Someone he wanted more.

His searching hand met empty sheets. He rolled over, reaching further, finding nothing but an empty bed and cold sheets and not the warm woman he was looking for. He cracked open an eyelid and found no one.

Now he was wide awake. 'Tora?' he called. But there was no answer, nothing but the soft hum of the air conditioner kicking in as the temperature rose with the sun outside.

'Tora,' he repeated, louder this time, on his feet now as he checked the bathroom and the living room. He pulled back the curtains in case she'd decided to take coffee out there so as not to waken him. Morning light poured into the room, and he squinted against the rising sun, but the terrace, like every other part of the suite, was empty.

She was gone, without so much as a word.

She was gone, before he was ready.

Before he was done with her.

He growled, a vein in his temple throbbing while his dark mood grew blacker by the minute.

Until he remembered with a jolt the revelations of yesterday and his black mood changed direction. He glanced at the clock. He had a meeting to get to.

He'd been angry when the lawyer had told him that he'd arranged it—too blindsided by the lawyer's revelations to think straight, too incensed that someone other than himself was suddenly pulling the strings of his life—but now he welcomed this meeting with this so-called vizier of Qajaran. Maybe he would have the answers to his questions.

Only then, when he was convinced, would he agree to take on this baby sister—no, half-sister—the product of a father who'd abandoned Rashid as a toddler, and a woman he'd taken as his lover.

Only then would he agree to take on guardianship of her, to take responsibility for her now that both her parents were dead, and to fill the void in her life, and wasn't that the richest thing of all?

Because how the hell was he supposed to fill a void in anyone's life when there'd been nobody to fill the void in his?

Thanks for that.

He cast one last glance back towards the rumpled bed as he headed to the shower, the bed that bore the tangled evidence of their lovemaking. How many times they'd come together in the dark night, he couldn't remember, only that every time he'd turned to her she'd been there, seemingly insatiable and growing bolder each time.

No wonder he'd been angry when he'd found her gone.

No wonder he'd felt short-changed.

But one night was what he'd wanted and it was better this way. She'd more than served her purpose. He'd lost himself in her and she'd blotted out the shock and pain for a while, but now he needed a clear head and no distractions. He thought back to the night that was. She'd been one hell of a distraction and he would have been hard pressed to send her on her way. It was better that she'd saved him the effort.

Kareem was not as Rashid had envisaged. He'd imagined someone called a vizier to be a small man, wiry and astute. But the man the lawyer introduced him to in his dark-timbered library was a tall, gentle-looking giant of indeterminate age who could have been anywhere from fifty to eighty. He looked the part of a wise man, perfectly at ease in his sandals and robes amongst a city full of men wearing suits and ties.

Kareem bowed when he was introduced to Rashid, his eyes wide. 'You are indeed your father's son.'

A tremor went down Rashid's spine. 'You knew my father?'

The older man nodded. 'I did, although our dealings have been few and far between of late. I knew you, too, as an infant. It is good to meet you again after all these years.'

The lawyer excused himself then, leaving the two men to talk privately.

'Why have you come?' Rashid asked, taking no time to get to the point. 'Why did you ask for this meeting?'

'Your father's death raises issues of which you

should be aware, even if I fear you may find them unpalatable.'

Rashid sighed. He was sick of all the riddles, but he was no closer today to believing that this man they were talking about actually was his father than when the lawyer had dropped that particular bombshell yesterday. 'You're going to have to try harder than that if you want to convince me. My father died when I was just a child.'

'That is what your father wanted you to believe,' the older man said.

'*Wanted* me to believe?'

'I take your point,' the vizier conceded, his big hands raised in surrender. 'It would be more correct to say that he wanted the entire world to believe he was dead. I did not mean to give the impression that he was singling you out.'

Rashid snorted. And that was supposed to be some kind of compensation?

'And my mother?' he snapped before the other man could continue. 'What of her? Is she similarly living out a life of gay abandon somewhere else in the world, having tossed her maternal responsibilities to the winds?'

The vizier shook his head. 'I almost wish I could tell you she was, but sadly no, your mother died while you were in infancy, as you are no doubt aware. I am sorry,' he said. 'I know this must be difficult for you, but there is more. Much more.'

Rashid waved the threat in those words away. 'I already know about this so-called sister, if that's what you're referring to.'

'Atiyah? Yes, she is on her way here now, I believe. But I was not referring to her.'

He frowned. 'Then what? In fact, why are you here? What do you have to do with my father's affairs anyway?'

The older man regarded him levelly, his eyes solemn. 'I know you were brought up,' he said, slowly and purposefully, as if sensing Rashid's discomfiture, 'believing your father to have been a humble tailor, killed in an industrial accident…' He paused, as if to check Rashid was still listening.

He was listening all right, although it was hard to hear with the thumping of his heart. Today he'd expected answers. Instead all he was getting was more of the madness.

'In actual case, your father was neither. Your father was a member of the Royal House of Qajar.' He paused again. 'Do you know much of Qajaran?'

Rashid closed his eyes. He knew the small desert country well enough—his work as a petroleum engineer had taken him there several times. It had a problematic economy, he was aware, like so many countries that he visited, not that he had paid this one much more attention than he paid any of them. He had learned early on in his career that it was better not to get involved in the affairs of state when one was a visiting businessman.

But for Rashid's father to have been a member of the House of Qajar—the father he'd believed to be nothing more than a tailor—then he must have been a member of the royal family…

The wheels of his mind started turning. 'So who was my father?'

'The Emir's nephew…' the vizier paused again '…and his chosen successor over his own son who he judged as being too self-centred and weak.'

His nephew? His chosen successor? 'But if what you say is true…' Rashid ground out the words, still not convinced by the story he was hearing '…why was he living here in Australia? What happened?'

The older man took a sip of his milk and returned it to its coaster, every move measured and calm and at odds with the turmoil Rashid was feeling inside.

'Your father was an accomplished polo player,' the vizier said, 'and while he was overseas competing in one of his polo competitions, the old Emir died suddenly.' He paused on a breath, the silence stretching out to breaking point. 'Some would say too suddenly, and, of course, there was some suggestion at the time that the timing was "convenient", but nothing could ever be proved. By the time your father had arrived home, the Emir's son had announced his ascension to the throne and moved the palace forces squarely behind himself. Your father knew nothing of this and was placed under house arrest the moment he returned to the palace. But your father was popular with the people and questions were inevitably asked about his disappearance—uncomfortable questions when all of Qajaran knew he was the favoured choice for Emir—and so Malik announced he was to be appointed special adviser to the Emir while deciding privately that it would be better to have him out of the way completely.'

'So they exiled him?'

'No. Malik was nowhere near that merciful. The plan was to kill him but make it look like an accident. A helicopter accident en route from the mountain palace to where the ceremony would take place.'

Air hissed through Rashid's teeth.

'Fortunately your father had a supporter in the palace. My predecessor could not stand back and let such a crime happen. They secreted bodies from the hospital morgue and when the time came, they parachuted to safety and the helicopter duly crashed, its cargo of dead burned beyond recognition, assumed to be the pilot and the true heir to the throne. Clothing from a small child was found in the wreckage, jackals assumed to have made off with the remains.'

Rashid felt chills down his spine. 'A small child,' he repeated. *'Me.'*

The vizier nodded. 'You. The new Emir was leaving nothing to chance. But your father's life came at a cost. To protect the lives of those who had saved him and his son, he had to swear he would never return to Qajaran, and he would live his life as an exile with a false identity. Your names were both changed, your histories altered, but, even so, as a father and son you would have been too recognisable together, and so, in order to keep you safe, he had to cut you free.'

Rashid's hands curled into fists. 'I grew up alone. I grew up thinking my father was dead."

The vizier was unapologetic. 'You grew up in safety. Had Malik suspected even one hint of your existence, he would have sent out his dogs and had you hunted down.'

Rashid battled to make sense of it all. 'But Malik died, what? Surely it's a year ago by now. Why did my father keep silent then? Why did he not move to claim the throne then if he was still alive?'

The older man shrugged and turned the palms

of his hands up to thc cciling. 'Because he had made a solemn promise never to return and he was a man of honour, a man of his word.'

'No, that doesn't cut it. He still could have told *me*! He could have sought me out. Why should I have been denied knowing my father was alive because of a promise he'd made to somebody else years ago?'

'I know.' The vizier exhaled on a sigh. 'Rashid, I am sorry to be the one to tell you this, but your father decided it was better that you never knew of your heritage. I sought him out after Malik died. I begged him to reach out to you—I begged him to let me reach out to you—but he refused. He said it was better that way, that you never knew the truth, that it couldn't hurt you any more than it already had. He made me promise not to contact you while he lived.'

Rashid shook his head, his jaw so tightly set he had to fight to squeeze the words out. 'So he decided to keep me in the dark—about everything. Even the fact my own father was still alive.'

'Don't you think it cost your father—to be cursed with only seeing his son from afar and searching thc papers for any hint of where you were and what you were doing? But he was proud of you and all that you achieved.'

'He had a funny way of showing it.'

'He saw all that you achieved by yourself and,

wrongly or rightly, he chose to let you remain on that path, unfettered by the responsibility he knew would come if you knew the truth.'

The sensation of scuttling insects started at the base of his neck and worked its way down his spine. He peered at the vizier through suspicious eyes and asked the questions he feared he already knew the answers to. 'What do you mean? What responsibility?'

'Don't you see? You are Qajaran's true and rightful ruler, Rashid. I am asking you to come back to Qajaran with me and claim the throne.'

CHAPTER FIVE

RASHID LAUGHED. He couldn't help but laugh, even though he'd half suspected something similar, but the old man was so fervent and the idea so preposterous. 'You can't be serious!'

'Please forgive me, but I am not in the habit of joking about such matters.'

Rashid got the impression the man was not in the habit of making jokes at all, the complete lack of humour in the vizier's response stopping Rashid's mirth dead. 'But I haven't lived in Qajaran since I was a boy, if what you say is true, because I certainly can't even remember a time when I did. I have visited it briefly two or three times since at the most. There must be someone better, someone more qualified?'

'There has been a power vacuum since Malik's death. A Council of Elders has taken over the basics of governing, but there is no clear direction and no one person to take responsibility. Qajaran needs a strong leader, and there can be no one more fitting than the son of the true successor. In the beginning, I know it is what your father wanted for you, to reclaim your birthright, even though with time he changed his mind and wished for you the freedom that he had found. He had made a life here, after all, and I think the longer he was away from Qajaran, the less connection he felt and the less your father felt he owed his homeland.'

'The father I never knew,' he said, not even trying to prevent the bitterness infusing his voice. 'If indeed he was my father. Why should I take your word that he was?'

The old man nodded. 'I would be concerned if you accepted too quickly the challenge that lies before you. I would think you are attracted to the concept of power, other than the benefit of our peoples.' He slipped a hand into the folds of his robes and pulled something from a pocket. 'Malik sought to destroy all likenesses of your father. This one survived.' He handed it to Rashid.

It was one of those old photo folders that opened like a card, the cardboard crinkled and dog-eared around the border but the picture inside still preserved. A photo of a man dressed dashingly in the Qajarese colours of orange, white and red, sitting proudly astride an Arab polo pony, a mallet casually slung over his shoulder as he posed for the camera.

'My God,' Rashid said, for he recognised his own features in the photograph—his own high cheekbones and forehead and the set of his jaw. The eyes the same dark blue. It could have been him sitting on that horse.

'You see it,' Kareem said. 'There is no denying it.' The old man leaned forward. 'Your country needs you, Rashid. Qajaran is at a crossroads. Thirty years of a ruler who wasted every opportunity unless it benefited him directly, thirty years of frittering the revenues that came from its industries and rich resources on follies and peccadilloes. It is more by good luck than good management that the economy of Qajaran has not been completely ruined. But now it is time to start building. There is a desperate need for strong leadership, education and reform.'

Rashid shook his head. 'Why would the people accept me as leader, when I am supposed to have died in a helicopter crash three decades ago? Why would they believe it is even me?'

'The people have long memories. Malik may have tried to wipe your father from the collective memory of the Qajarese people, but never could he wipe the love of him from their hearts. Truly, you would be welcomed back.'

'When I am supposed to be dead? How does that work?'

'Your body was never found, assumed to be taken by the desert beasts, which means there is doubt. The people of Qajaran are in desperate need of a miracle. The return of you to Qajaran would be that miracle.'

Rashid shook his head. 'This is madness. I am a petroleum engineer. That is my job—that is what I do.'

'But you were born Qajarese. You were born to rule. That is in your blood.'

Rashid stood, his legs too itchy to remain seated any longer, and crossed to a window, watching the traffic and the pedestrians rushing by in the street below. They all had somewhere to go, somewhere to be. Nobody was stopping them and telling them that their lives up till now had been founded on a lie, and that they must become someone they had never in their wildest nightmares thought they would be. Nobody was telling them they had a tiny sister they were now responsible for—let alone a nation full of people for whom they were now responsible.

He shook his head. He didn't do family. The closest he had ever come to having family was his three friends, his desert brothers, Zoltan, Bahir and Kadar, their friendship forged at university in the crucible of shared proximity and initial animosity, all of them outcasts, all of them thrust together as a kind of sick joke—the four had hated each other on sight—only for the joke to backfire when the four became friends and the 'Sheikhs'

Caïque', as their rowing four was nicknamed, won every race they ran.

And even though his three desert brothers had found matches and were starting their own broods of children, it didn't mean he had to follow suit.

He had no desire for family. Even less now given he'd learned his father had lived all those years and hadn't bothered to let him know—his own son!

And what was a nation but the worst kind of family, large, potentially unruly and dependent.

He turned suddenly. Faced the man who had brought him this horror. 'Why should I do this? Why should I take this on?'

Kareem nodded. 'I have read widely of you and seen your long list of achievements and your powers of negotiation when dealing with disparate parties. You would come eminently qualified to the task of Emir.'

Rashid shook his head, and the older man held up one broad hand. 'But yes, this is no job application. This goes beyond mere qualifications. Your father was the chosen Emir before circumstances forced him into exile. You are his heir. It is therefore your duty.'

Rashid's blood ran cold. 'My duty? I thought you said I had a choice.'

And Kareem looked hard into his eyes. 'The

choice is not mine to give. I am saying you have this duty. Your choice is whether you accept it.'

Duty.

He was not unfamiliar with the concept. His best friends were no strangers to duty. He had seen Zoltan take on the quest for the throne of Al-Jirad. Rashid had done his brotherly duty and had ridden together with him and Bahir and Kadar across the desert to rescue Princess Aisha, and later to snatch her sister, Princess Marina, from the clutches of Mustafa. He had always done his duty.

But never had he imagined that duty would be so life-changing—so unpalatable—for himself. Because if he did this thing, his life would undergo a seismic shift. He would never be truly free again. And if he didn't, he would be failing in his duty.

Duty. Right now the most cursed of four-letter words.

'What I tell you is not easy for a man to absorb or accept,' Kareem said. 'I can only ask that you will come and see the country for yourself. Bring Atiyah, for it is her heritage and birthright too.'

'You want me to willingly turn up on the door-step of a place that was so happy to see my father and me dead? You expect me to take an infant into that environment?'

'Malik is gone. You have nothing to fear from him or his supporters now. Please, you must come, Rashid. Come and feel the ancient sand of our country between your toes and let it run through your fingers. See the sunrise and sunset over the desert and maybe then you will feel the heart of Qajaran beating in your soul.'

'I'll come,' Rashid said, his head knowing what he had to do, his gut twisting tighter than steel cable in spite of it. 'For now that is all I am promising.'

The vizier nodded. 'For now, it is enough. Let me call the lawyer back in and we will make the arrangements.'

'What can they be doing in there?' Tora said as she gave up pacing the lawyer's waiting room and sat down in the chair alongside her boss. She had to pace because every now and then her lack of sleep would catch up with her and she'd find herself yawning. 'Whatever can be taking so long?' she said, trying not to sound too irate so that she didn't disturb the infant in the capsule alongside. She'd had barely enough time to get home to shower and change and pack her things, before she'd met Sally at Flight Nanny's office and they'd headed off together to pick up the baby from the foster home where she'd been looked after for the last few days, only for them to have been kept sitting and waiting so long that the baby would soon need another feed.

Her boss twisted her watch around her wrist. 'I don't know, but I can't stay much longer. I've got a meeting with Steve's doctors in less than an hour.'

'I'm sure it won't be too long now,' the middle-aged receptionist assured them when Sally asked how long it would be, before disappearing to fetch refreshments.

The baby started fussing then and Tora reached down to soothe her. She was a cherub. With black curls and dark eyes with long sooty lashes and a tiny Cupid's-bow mouth, it was obvious that she'd grow up to be a beauty. But right now she was a tiny vulnerable infant without a mother or a father—or anyone who seemed to care what happened to her.

The baby wasn't about to be placated and became more restless, her little fisted hands protesting, and Tora plucked her out of the capsule to prop against her shoulder so she could rub her back, swaying from side to side in her seat as she did so.

She smiled as she cuddled the infant close, enjoying the near new baby smell. It was unusual to have such a young infant to take care of. Most of Flight Nanny's charges were small children who needed to be ferried interstate or overseas between divorced parents who were either too busy with their careers to travel with their children, or who simply preferred to avoid any contact with the other party, even if only to hand the children over. Those cases could be sad enough.

But an infant who'd been left orphaned, that was beyond tragic. That was cruel.

'You poor sweetheart,' she said as she rocked the tiny bundle in her arms, her heart breaking a little at the injustice of it all.

Sally shifted in her seat and Tora could feel the tension emanating from her friend and colleague. Something was seriously wrong. 'How is Steve?' she ventured, once the baby had settled a little, scared to ask, even more scared for the answer.

Her boss grimaced and it occurred to Tora that Sally had aged ten years in the last couple of weeks. 'He's struggling. There's a chance they won't be able get his condition stabilised enough for the flight to Germany.' She looked up then and Tora saw the desperation in her eyes, desperation laced with a flash of hope. 'Look, Tora, I didn't want to ask—I really wanted to wait for you to say something—but how did you get on with your cousin last night? Did he give you any idea when the estate might be finalised and that settlement might come through?'

And Tora's heart plunged to the floor. There was damned good reason she hadn't wanted to come to work today and it wasn't just that she'd hardly had any sleep. Without the funds from her parents' estate, she'd have nothing to lend to Sally and Steve, funds they'd been counting on to pay for his medical transport and his treatment overseas. And she'd really wanted some time to explore any other ways of raising the money before she had to come clean on the fact that the promised funds were never going to materialise—not from that particular source. 'Ah,' she said with false brightness, as if she'd only just remembered, 'I wanted to talk to you about that.'

Sally crossed her arms and Tora could see her fingernails clawing into her arms. 'Damn. I knew I shouldn't have asked you that. I don't think I could bear to hear bad news today.'

'Oh, no,' Tora lied, doing her utmost to smile. 'Nothing like that. Just paperwork and more paperwork.' She shrugged. 'You know how it goes with these things. I'm really hoping it gets resolved soon.'

Sally glanced at her watch. 'Well, sorry, but I'm going to have to leave you with some more paperwork if I'm going to make this appointment.' She reached into her satchel and pulled out a folder that she left on the seat behind her as she rose. 'I'm really sorry to leave you like this when we still don't know all the details. Will you be okay to handle everything yourself?'

'Hey, I'll be fine. If you're going to be disappearing offshore soon,' she said, trying to stay positive and not wanting to dwell on how big that 'if' was right now if she couldn't secure the funds to make it happen, 'we're all going to have to get used to doing more paperwork here at home. Don't worry, I'll email you when I know where this baby is going and scan all the documentation for you before we go anywhere. You just worry about you and Steve right now.'

Sally smiled, giving Tora a kiss on the cheek as she bent down to pick up her bag. 'Thanks.' She curled a fingertip under the baby's tiny hand. 'Look after this little poppet, okay?'

'You bet. Now get going. And give my love to Steve.'

Sally was gone by the time the receptionist returned with her iced tea, and Tora's was half drunk when the door to the office opened then, and an older gent with bushy eyebrows and a shock of white hair peeked out. 'Ah, Joan,' he said. 'We're ready for our guests now.' He looked at Tora and the bundle perched over her shoulder.

'I'm sorry,' she said, 'but Sally Barnes couldn't stay.'

'I quite understand,' he said kindly. 'This has all taken rather longer than we expected. Thank you for being so patient, Ms Burgess. Do come in. It's time for the little one to meet her guardian.'

She stood up with the baby in her arms, and the lawyer surprised her by shoving the folder Sally had left under his arm, before picking up both the baby capsule and baby bag.

'Gentlemen,' he said as he shouldered open the door and ushered her into the room, 'here is Atiyah at last, along with Ms Victoria Burgess, who comes to us highly qualified from Flight Nanny, the number one Australian business that transports unaccompanied children all around the world. Victoria will be caring for Atiyah and accompanying you both to Qajaran.'

Tora raised her eyebrows as she digested the news. So that was where she was headed? That would be a first. She'd been to many ports in Europe and Asia but so far she'd never had an assignment that took her to the smaller Middle East states. A tall, gentle-looking man wearing Arabic robes came towards her, a warm smile on his creased face as he looked benevolently down upon the child in her arms. He reached a finger to her downy cheek and uttered something in Arabic that sounded very much like a blessing to Tora. If this man was the tiny Atiyah's guardian, she was sure she would be in good hands.

'Excuse me,' he said with a bow. 'I will inform the pilot we will be on standby.' And with a swish of his robes, he left the room.

'Victoria,' someone else said from a chair in

the corner of the room behind her, in a voice as dry and flat as a desert in summer—a voice she recognised as one that had vibrated its way into her bones last night with desire but that now set off electric shocks up and down her spine with fear. 'Most people would shorten that to *Tori*, wouldn't they?'

Please, God, no, she prayed, but when she looked around, it was him all right. He rose from his chair then, the man she'd spent the many dark hours of last night with naked, the man now looking at her with storm-swept eyes. Her heart lurched and she clutched the baby in her arms tighter, just to be sure she didn't drop her.

'I don't know,' she said, trying and not sure she was succeeding in keeping the tremor from her voice. 'Is it relevant?'

The lawyer looked strangely at Rashid, questions clear in his eyes. 'Yes,' he said, 'what does it matter? Come, Rashid, and see your sister and your new charge.'

His sister? Surely that didn't mean what she thought it meant? And Tora felt the cold tea in her stomach turn to sludge.

He hadn't been in a rush to get up—he might have agreed to go to Qajaran and take the child with him, but he was in no desperate hurry to meet her. He was glad he'd hung back in his chair now, glad of the time to let incredulity settle into cold, indisputable truth.

Because it was her.

The woman who'd stolen away from his bed like a thief in the night.

The woman he'd never expected to see again.

She looked almost the same as she had last night in the bar, in a beige short-sleeved shirt and hair that he now knew fell heavy like a curtain of silk when pulled out of that damned abomination of a bun, but with black trousers this time, covering legs he could still feel knotted around his back as he drove into her.

She looked almost the same in that bland mouse-like uniform she wore that he knew hid a firebrand underneath.

And it seemed that twenty-four hours of being blindsided didn't show any signs of letting up yet.

'Rashid?' the lawyer prompted. 'Don't you want to meet your sister?'

Not particularly, he thought, and least of all now when she was being cradled in the arms of a woman he hadn't begun to forget, though he supposed he should look interested enough to take a look.

He rose to his feet. Was it his imagination or did the woman appear to shift backwards? No, he realised, it wasn't his imagination. There was fear in her eyes even though the angle of her chin remained defiant. She was scared of him and trying not to show it. Scared because he knew what the nanny got up to in the night time.

She should be worried.

In spite of himself, he got closer. Close enough that the scent of the woman he'd spent the last night with curled into his senses, threatening to undo the control he was so desperately trying to hang onto. Didn't he have enough to contend with right now—a father who'd removed himself from Rashid's life, only to leave him this tiny legacy, a country that was floundering where he was expected to take up the reins—without a woman who had the power to short his senses and make him forget? He needed his wits about him now, more than ever, not this siren whose body even now seemed to call to him.

He shifted his head back out of range, and concentrated instead on the squirming bundle in her arms. Black hair and chubby arms and a screwed-up face. Definitely a baby. He didn't know a lot about babies, but then he'd never expected to need to.

'Would you like to hold her?' the woman he knew as Tora ventured, her voice tight, as if she was having trouble getting the words out.

It was his turn to take a step back. 'No.'

'She won't break.'

'I said no.' And neither, when he thought about it, did he want this woman holding her, let alone accompanying them to Qajaran. Not that he was about to take the child himself. He turned to the lawyer. 'Is there no one else you could have found for this role?'

The woman blinked up at him, her brown eyes as cold as marble. Too bad. Did she expect him to greet her like a long-lost friend? Not likely.

'Excuse me?' the lawyer asked.

'Someone more suitable to take care of Atiyah. Couldn't you find someone better to take care of my sister?'

'Ms Burgess comes to us highly qualified. She has an exemplary record with Flight Nanny. Would you like to see her credentials?'

'That's not necessary.' He'd already seen her credentials, in glorious satin-skinned detail, and they qualified her for a different type of position entirely from the one she was required for now.

'If you have some kind of problem—' she started.

'Yes, I have "some kind of problem", Ms Burgess. Perhaps we should discuss this in private and I'll spell it out for you?'

The lawyer looked at them nervously. 'If you excuse me, a moment, I'll see how Kareem is going,' and he too was gone.

Rashid took a deep breath as he strode back towards the wall of windows.

'What are you doing here? How did you find me?'

'What? I didn't find you. I was asked by my boss to take this job on. I didn't know you had anything to do with Atiyah.'

'You expect me to believe it's some kind of coincidence?'

'You can believe what you like. I was retained to care for Atiyah on her journey to wherever it is that she is going. Frankly, I'd forgotten all about you already.'

His teeth ground together. Forgotten about him already? In his world, women had always been temporary, but he'd been the one to decide when he'd had enough. He'd been the one to forget, and it grated…

'So you're a qualified child-care worker?'

'That's my primary qualification, yes, though I have diplomas in school-aged education and childhood health care along with some language skills as well.'

'You are forgetting about your *other* skills,' he growled, his lip curling as he looked out of the window, still resentful at a world going on about its business while his life didn't resemble a train that had merely changed direction, his life was on a train that had jumped tracks, and he wasn't sure he liked where it was headed.

'They're hardly relevant,' she said behind him, and around and between her words he could hear the sounds of the baby, staccato bursts of cackles and cries, and then a zipper being undone.

He spun around, angry that she seemed oblivious to the impossibility of the situation, to see her sitting down, the baby in her lap as she dripped milk from a small bottle onto her upturned wrist before putting the bottle to the baby's mouth, looking every part the quintessential mother with child.

That was a laugh. She was no Madonna. It didn't matter what she was wearing or what she was doing, he could still see her naked. He could still remember the way she'd bucked beneath him as she'd come apart in his arms.

'Impossible!' he said, and even the baby was startled, her big eyes open wide, her little hands jerking upwards, fingers splayed. 'This cannot work.'

'Hold it down,' she said, rocking the child in her arms. 'Do you think I like the situation any more than you do?'

'I want another carer.'

'Why?'

Because I don't trust myself with you. 'Because

a woman like you is not fit to look after an innocent child.'

She laughed. 'A woman like me? What kind of woman is that, exactly?'

'A woman who goes whoring in the night—picking up men in bars and sleeping with them.'

She smiled up at him and he felt his ire rise. 'But a *man* who goes whoring in the night—picking up women and inviting them back to his hotel room—he is perfectly qualified to be that child's guardian. Is that what you are saying?'

'This is not about me.'

'Clearly not, or there might be a double standard at work, don't you think?'

Frustration tangled in his gut. He hated that she had seen through his arguments but he could hardly tell her the real reason—that he needed more than ever right now to be able to think clearly, without his brain being distracted with replays of last night every time he looked at her. Why couldn't she see that he didn't want her—that this would not work? 'I want somebody else to care for Atiyah!'

'There is nobody else. All Flight Nanny's employees are busy on other assignments.'

'I don't want you coming with us.'

'Do you think for a moment that I want to come? As soon as I realised it was you, I wanted to sink through a hole in the floor. So don't worry,

I'm not looking for a repeat of last night's little adventure. I'm not here because of you. I'm here to take care of the baby, nothing more.'

A brief knock on the door interrupted his words, and Kareem entered with a bow, and there was no way their visitor couldn't have heard her words or misinterpreted the tone in which they were delivered. 'A thousand pardons for the interruption, but the plane will be ready to leave in two hours.'

And Tora looked up at Rashid. 'So, do you want to tell everyone why you'd prefer to find another carer, or shall I?'

Kareem looked to him expectantly, his placid features betraying only the barest hint of surprise, and Rashid cursed the woman under his breath. But he was out of time and out of options, and, besides, what was the worst that could happen? She'd accompany them to Qajaran and then her role would be complete and she would be on the next flight home and he would be rid of the constant reminders of their night of passion together, rid of the distraction of a woman who had turned an already upside-down world spinning through another three hundred and sixty degrees in the course of one night. He could hardly wait. 'I expected someone older,' he muttered, 'but I suppose this one will just have to do.'

CHAPTER SIX

BLUFF WAS A beautiful thing, when it came off.

Tora got the baby capsule secured and sank into the buttery leather of the limousine and took a deep, calming breath. Because she'd done it, she'd saved the assignment. Sally would have been devastated if she'd lost this contract—and Tora would have found it next to impossible to explain how she'd let it happen. How did one go about explaining that you'd inadvertently slept with the client after meeting them in a bar the night before your assignment? It didn't bear thinking about.

But Rashid had given himself away when he'd asked to speak to her in private. Clearly he wasn't too keen on sharing the details of exactly why he deemed her unsuitable to care for his sister. So sure, she wasn't about to go advertising the way she'd behaved last night, but it seemed she wasn't the only one with a secret to keep.

Was he married? Was that his problem? She hadn't thought to ask last night. One night he'd offered and she'd taken it, no questions asked. And maybe it didn't reflect well on her, but last night had been just about perfect as far as she was concerned, at least until she'd entered that lawyer's office today and found him lying in wait and in judgement.

He'd been a different man last night. Bold. Decisive. He'd been angry, as she had been—and she'd felt it with his every move, his every thrust. Whereas today he seemed to be on the defensive.

What was that about?

Kareem climbed into the front seat beside the driver and turned to her. 'Do you have everything you need, Ms Burgess?'

She nodded. 'Thank you,' she said as she checked the sleeping infant, a tiny milky bubble swirling in the corner of her mouth. 'We're both very comfortable.'

Kareem nodded. 'Then we shall go.'

Tora looked around. 'Where is Rashi—? Where is Atiyah's guardian?'

'His Excellency is travelling separately. He will meet us at the airport.'

She nodded dumbly and settled back into her seat as the car cruised away. *His Excellency?*

Exactly who had she spent last night with?

He was stuck with her now. At least for the next however many hours it took to fly to Qajaran.

Only a few hours, Rashid reasoned as the driver made his way towards the coast, and then she would be on her way home again. It should be easy, given he'd only known her a few hours, but the way they'd spent them, and the way she'd left so abruptly, was it any wonder that he was still aching for more?

But he didn't want more, he told himself. He didn't need the distraction. He didn't need to be reminded of his wanting her every time he saw her. He didn't need to know she was close enough to take.

A few hours? God, already they felt too long.

Rashid had the driver stop just before the road turned to the right along the cliff face, and climbed out into the full force of the wind blowing off the Pacific Ocean. In front of them the ocean waves pounded against the rocky cliffs, sending the boiling spray high into the air, while to the left sprawled a cemetery as big as several city blocks, the marble headstones and funerary ornaments marching up the hillside to the silent blare of the angels' trumpets.

It was a wild place, elemental, the blue-skied summer day's temperature turned on its head as the tiny sparkling droplets of sea water drifted down and conspired with the wind to suck your body heat away. He welcomed it as he turned up the collar of his linen jacket.

It was the perfect place to forget about her.

He started walking, gravel crunching underfoot, towards the place the lawyer had marked for him on a map. He didn't need to look at the map again, the paths were wide and the way clear, and before long he could make out the fresh mound of earth that marked the grave where his father and his lover had been laid to rest.

He stood there, at the foot of the grave with its two white markers, feeling hollow inside. He had no flowers. He wasn't here to shed tears. He wasn't even sure why he'd come, only that he'd been compelled to visit, just once before he left this country.

Wasn't sure if he'd come to pay his respects to a father who'd cast him adrift when he was but a child, or to rail against him and demand to know why he'd abandoned him. Sure, he'd heard the lawyer's version of events, and he'd heard Kareem's, but surely he'd had a right to hear it for himself?

Surely he'd had a right to ask whether his father had ever thought of him on his birthday or whether he'd ever felt a hole in his heart where his son should have been?

He stood there, battered by the breeze caused by sea slamming into rock, until in the end Rashid knew there were no answers for him here.

Yet still he stayed a while, a silent sentinel, while the wild wind tugged at his jacket and hair and the spray from the crashing waves on the cliffs behind rained like mist over him, until finally he said in a gravelly voice to a father he couldn't remember, 'I will never understand why you did what you did. And I will never forgive you.'

And then he turned and walked away.

The jet was whisper quiet, piercing the air with the maximum of speed and the minimum of fuss or inconvenience to its passengers. Tora sat wrapped in one of the enormous leather seats, still shell-shocked. She'd travelled business class with a rock star's child once, and that had seemed luxurious after usually being consigned to economy with the children, but this was more than luxurious, this was sumptuous.

Timber-panelled walls with gold trim, plum-coloured leather seats that reclined and spun and laid flat and looked more suited to a lounge room than a plane, and opulent carpets in vermilion on gold on the floor, with enough space in between the seats to swing an entire herd of cats, while fresh frangipani placed discreetly in tiny vials around the cabin walls perfumed the air.

But then, this wasn't business class and it wasn't the only reason for her shell shock. This was the royal jet of Qajaran, and her tiny charge was some kind of princess.

What did that make Rashid?

He sat across the aisle in the row ahead, deep in conversation with Kareem. She could hear their voices every now and then, Kareem's measured and calm tones, interspersed with Rashid's arguments, though she couldn't make out what they were discussing but could see that whatever they were talking about was raising temperatures—Rashid's at least. She could make out his profile—strong lines even down to the lips on a mouth that was now snapping out words. Lips that she knew could give an inordinate amount of pleasure. She squirmed a little in her seat as she watched him, remembering, tingling in places that shouldn't be tingling right now.

God, she was kidding herself if she could forget, but it would be better for everyone if she could put those particular memories aside for however long this assignment took.

And then he turned, and caught her watching him, and she held her breath as a tremor zigzagged down her spine, unable to tear her eyes away as his dark eyes gleamed and pinned her to her seat. Then he said something short to the man beside her before turning away and severing the bonds between them.

Breath whooshed out of her in a rush as she felt his hold on her release. She took a couple of restorative breaths. What was that about?

Why had he looked at her that way, not with

anger or resentment exactly, but with eyes that were so cold, hard and calculated?

Beside her, Atiyah gurgled happily in the bassinet strapped to the seat, and she blinked, focusing on what was important here. Not Rashid and his clear preference that she'd disappeared into the past and stayed there when she left his bed this morning, but this tiny baby.

Tora smiled as she leaned over the bassinet. She couldn't help but smile when she looked at Atiyah's face with her big dark eyes and tiny button nose and the pink lips busy making shapes and testing sounds. Likewise, she couldn't help but feel the tug on her heartstrings when she thought about how she'd grow up never knowing her mother or father. It was so unfair. It was wrong.

She should be smiling at two months. She probably would, if she saw her mother's face. For now, she looked up with those big eyes at Tora as if everything was new again, as it must seem to her.

It was so unfair to lose her parents just when the world was coming into focus and making sense. She needed stability now, and people to love her. Hopefully, once she was in Qajaran with a regular carer, she would remember how to smile.

Maybe Rashid might even take an interest in her by then. He'd shown precious little interest to date, treating her more as a parcel he had to convey rather than as his tiny sister. He just didn't seem interested.

What was with that?

But then, he didn't look like a man who smiled much. He seemed angry about everything.

The baby cooed and closed her eyes and took a deep breath, settling back for another brief nap. Tora reclined her chair a little and sat sideways, almost envying Atiyah's ability to turn off the outside world. She watched her sleep, the low drone of the plane's engines like white noise, and the wide chair so comfortable, and yawned, feeling her own eyelids grow heavier.

'There is just one more issue that is of concern,' Kareem said, after a welcome pause that Rashid had taken to meaning their business was over, 'that must be discussed.'

'Why, when I still haven't agreed to take on the throne?' Kareem had gone through page after page of notes to explain the path to the throne and the coronation that must take place if he did agree, while going on to outline not only the history of the tiny but resource-rich state but the current challenges, both internal and external, that it faced, and right now Rashid's head felt as if it were about to explode.

Surely there couldn't be anything else?

'I am sorry, Excellency, but, now that we are on our way home, there is a question over Atiyah, and her place in the royal family.'

Rashid shook his head. This one at least was a no-brainer. 'She is my father's daughter. She is my sister. What possible question could there be?'

The vizier nodded. 'Both true. However, the fact remains that thirty years ago your father was supposed to have been killed in a helicopter crash. A body was recovered and accepted as his. Questions will be asked if you claim Atiyah is your father's daughter. Uncomfortable questions. The people will want to know where he has been all that time and why he abandoned them to their fate with his cousin while he was enjoying his life with a young mistress the other side of the world…'

'You said he had to promise not to return!'

'He did. But you had problems accepting that truth. Magnify that doubt by the population of Qajaran…' He paused. 'And of course, there are pockets still loyal to the memory of Malik. They will not want to believe this could be true. Is it not better to let history lie so they cannot dispute? Is it not better to let the population continue to believe your father died in that helicopter crash? Your coming home will still be the miracle they need—the child who miraculously survived and was spirited away to safety.'

Rashid's head was pounding. His life was getting more complicated by the minute. 'What does it even matter?' he growled. 'I'm Atiyah's legal guardian, aren't I?'

'Technically, yes.'

'Only "technically"?'

'Guardianship of infants and minors by unmarried men is not recognised under Qajarese law.'

'So? I don't even know if I'm going to be staying all that long.'

'It is an inconvenience, I know, but Atiyah will not be able to share your palace quarters if she is not officially acknowledged as part of your family.'

He sighed, pressing his head back deep into his head rest. He hadn't asked to be this child's guardian but it was pretty clear that he could not let her be whisked away to God knew where to be looked after for however long this thing took. 'Then what can be done?'

'There is a way.'

'Which is?'

'Adopt Atiyah. Claim her as your own, if only in public.'

Rashid sat back in his seat, his mind reeling. What was happening to him that this proposal sounded half reasonable? Minute by minute he could feel the weight of the responsibility of a tiny desert kingdom pressing down on his shoulders, and he wondered, when it all came down to it, how much choice he really had.

'All right,' he said at last. 'What needs to be done?'

'Oh, it is but a stroke of the pen. I can handle it if you so desire.'

'Fine. Do it, then.'

If he thought that was an end to the matter and he could finally close his eyes and relax, he was sadly mistaken. Kareem was still there, watching him. 'What?' he snapped.

'There is but one *tiny* formality.'

There would be. Rashid rubbed a hand over his jaw. 'And that is?'

'To adopt in Qajaran, one must be married.'

'What? Why the hell didn't you say that before? It's pointless, then.'

'There is no one you have in mind to take for your wife?'

'No! Surely there is another way?'

'There is no other way.'

'Great. And you've only just discovered this now, when we're already on our way to Qajaran?'

Kareem bowed. 'My apologies, Excellency, this is a situation without precedent—I was hoping there would be something in the texts that might provide some comfort on this issue, but no. The texts are clear—only married couples can adopt. Perhaps, if there is no one you can suggest, I might be able to procure a suitable candidate on arrival in Qajaran City?'

'You? Find me a wife?'

'If only as a temporary measure, if it pleases you.' He raised one pen-laden hand as if he were being perfectly reasonable and Rashid only had to see it. 'It would simply be a matter of convenience.'

'And then?'

'And then you can divorce the woman and she can go her own way and you would retain custody of Atiyah. Please be assured when I say that both marriage and divorce in Qajaran are arrangements that require not much more than the stroke of a pen.'

'You said the same about adoption,' Rashid growled, 'and yet it seems needlessly complicated.'

The older man had the grace to smile ruefully as he held up his hands. 'Some strokes of the pen are more straightforward than others, but if you want to protect Atiyah, this is the only way.'

Rashid found it hard to argue the point, put like that, but he had his doubts about Kareem choosing him a bride, for however long or short this marriage was to be. Just because he had never entertained the concept of marriage was no reason to hand over the responsibility of selecting a wife. 'This wife I need—what would she be required to do?'

'She would have to perform as your wife in the public arena. She would have to be by your side during the coronation, if you go through with it, of course. Similarly at any public appearances where a mixed audience is in attendance—'

'And night times, Kareem. What would she be expected to do then?'

And for the first time Kareem looked somewhere approaching nonplussed. 'A wife populates her husband's bed at night. What else would you expect of her?'

'Of course,' Rashid said, frowning for added gravitas, while absolutely determined now that Kareem would have no part of choosing him a wife. Someone to escort him to official functions was one thing, but someone to take to his bed—only he decided who that would be. 'That is how it should be.'

'So you would like me to arrange a wife?'

'No. That won't be necessary. I've got a better idea.' One that would show a certain woman that when he said he did not want her for his sister's carer she should pay heed, that she was far better off agreeing with him and vanishing from his life just as silently as she had done from his bed this morning, or he might just think they had unfinished business.

A temporary wife to populate his bed could be some kind of compensation for this whole crazy scenario.

'Perhaps,' Kareem prompted, 'you would care to share this better idea?'

Rashid suddenly swung his head around and caught Tora watching him and he smiled.

Because although it seemed the train his life was on hadn't just changed tracks, it had changed planets, for the first time in a mad day he felt as if he was back in the driver's seat.

'I'm going to marry Victoria.'

'Ms Burgess?' Kareem forgot how to be serene and fairly spluttered. 'When you were so against her caring for Atiyah?'

'I know,' he said, unable to explain because the reason he was against her coming was the reason that made her most qualified to be his temporary wife. 'It's perfect.'

CHAPTER SEVEN

'TIRED, MS BURGESS?'

Tora came to with a start to see Rashid leaning down before her, as attentive and seemingly caring as any of the flight attendants as he held what looked like a pot of coffee in one hand and a cup in the other, and it wasn't the coffee she could smell. He hadn't bothered to exchange two words to her since she'd walked out of that lawyer's office in Sydney. Something was definitely up.

'I must have dozed off,' she said warily, sitting up straighter and checking her watch. No, she'd only been asleep a few minutes and one glance towards the bassinet beside her was enough to tell her that Atiyah was still sleeping, her little arms flung back either side of her head.

'Anyone would think you've been working too hard.'

Her eyes snapped back to his. There was a cunning gleam there that had her on alert. 'Anyone except you, you mean.'

'Come, come, Ms Burgess,' he said as he put the coffee down on a small table. 'I brought you coffee.'

She looked around the cabin but it was deserted, the cabin crew all discreetly tucked away wherever it was they waited between being called upon. Even Kareem had disappeared somewhere. 'Yes, I can see. What's with that? Did you sack all the flight attendants or something?'

He smiled as he swivelled the chair in front of her around and sat down, though she sensed danger in the curve of his lips. She tucked her feet under her chair. Even with the room between the seats his long legs ventured way too far into her space for her liking. 'I have something I need to discuss with you, something that might work to our mutual benefit.'

Her eyes shuttered down. Yeah, right. 'I told you I wasn't here for you. I am here for Atiyah, nothing more.'

'You have a suspicious mind.'

'You have a transparent one.'

He shook his head. 'This is not about bedding you.' He hesitated there, and she wondered what had gone unsaid. 'This concerns Atiyah.'

'How?'

He leaned forward. 'For reasons you don't need to know about, I need to adopt Atiyah.'

She looked across at him blankly. 'And how does that concern me?'

'In order to adopt, under some quaint Qajarese law, I must be married.'

She swallowed down on a lurch in her stomach because this could in no way mean what crazy idea ventured first into her mind. 'I repeat,' she said, schooling her voice to level and wishing her heart rate would also take heed, 'how does that concern me?'

'It's not for long, it's just a temporary thing. A mere formality, really, and then in a matter of months we can be divorced.'

There was that lurch again, but this time there was no misreading his words. 'We?'

'Well, you and me.'

She blinked, hoping it covered the jolt to her senses that came with his answer. 'There is no you and me.'

'There doesn't have to be, not in any real sense. All I need is a wife. Someone to play the role of Atiyah's mother temporarily. Kareem tells me the marriage must last twelve months to ensure the adoption satisfies the laws of Qajaran, but that's only if I decide to stay. Otherwise, it might be over within a week.' He smiled, as if he were asking her nothing more than the time of day. 'Like I said, it's just a formality.'

'But a year! There's a chance I have to be married to you for an entire year!'

'If it happens. But you would not need to stay in Qajaran all that time. Once the formalities were over, you could go home.'

She looked at the coffee he had poured for her. She liked coffee, but right now she felt the need for something a whole lot stronger.

She licked her lips. ‘Who are you?’

‘I told you. My name is Rashid.’

She shook her head. ‘No. I met someone called Rashid in a hotel bar. He was just a man. An angry man wanting to let off steam the way men do. But you—’ She looked around. ‘You fly in a plane with a golden crown for a crest, you have staff that bow and scrape and seem to wait on your every word and call you Excellency. So, Rashid, who are you, that you think it is perfectly reasonable to ask a near stranger to marry you so you can divorce them when it suits?’

His eyes left her face, to wander a scorching trail down her body, lingering on her breasts before venturing lower. He smiled. ‘Near stranger?’ he questioned, his voice husky around the edges, rasping against her very soul. ‘We are hardly strangers.’

She crossed her arms and legs to stop the tingling under her skin, relieved when his gaze once again found her face. ‘You don’t know me and I sure as hell don’t know anything about you.’

‘I am not asking the world, merely for a few weeks of your time and then you can go home.’

‘I said I wouldn’t sleep with you again and I sure as hell won’t marry you.’

'Nobody said anything about sleeping with me. You served a purpose last night, but now I'm looking for something else.'

She laughed, not sure whether to be offended or not. It was so mad, she had no other option but to laugh. 'Well, as attractive as you make your proposal sound, that I pretend to be your wife, no thank you.' She glanced at the baby and assured herself she would be all right for a minute or two more, before she pushed herself up to stand. Maybe if she headed for the bathroom, it might put a stop to this ridiculous conversation. But Rashid rose too, stepping sideways and blocking her path. 'Excuse me,' she said. 'I need to use the bathroom.'

'Not yet. You haven't heard what I'm offering in return.'

'I don't need to, to say no. You made it very clear when we were in Sydney that you didn't want me to be here at all. You made it clear that you wanted nothing more to do with me and that's fine, because I don't plan on sticking around any longer than I have to in order to do this job. As soon as I hand this child over to whoever is going to be her carer in Qajaran—because I assume from your lack of interest it won't be you—I'll be heading home.'

His eyes narrowed. 'Come now, Ms Burgess,

how can you say no when there is so much on offer?'

'Like what?'

'Like an all-expenses-paid holiday in Qajaran, complete with a bird's-eye view of a possible coronation and all the festivities surrounding it, along with a return flight home in the royal jet.'

A shiver ran down her spine. 'Whose coronation?'

'Mine.'

Ri—ight. So that was it. She did her best not to sway on her feet. Did her best not to look stunned. 'So you're kind of king-in-waiting, then?'

He nodded. 'You could put it that way. Qajaran is currently without an Emir. Apparently I am next in line to the throne, if I agree to take the role on.'

A kind of king. Well, that was kind of funny when she'd thought he'd looked like a god on the bed only this morning. A demotion almost, and that thought almost brought a smile to her face when there should be none.

She shook her head. 'Sorry, not interested.'

'How much, then?'

'Excuse me?'

'How much would it take? Everyone has their price—name it.'

She shook her head. She must be dreaming.

That or she'd woken up on some bizarre television game show. Any minute now and they'd be cutting to a commercial break for disposable nappies or dishwashing liquid. 'I told you, I'm not interested.'

'Name it!'

She sucked in air. She didn't want to do this. She didn't want to spend a moment longer in this man's company than she had to. The night she'd spent with him was too fresh, too raw in her mind, the passions he'd unleashed in her still making her senses hum at his proximity as if his mere presence was enough to switch them on—but then she thought about the amount her cousin had stolen from her and the money she had assured Sally she would find…

He wouldn't say yes, she told herself, there was no way he'd say yes, but if he really wanted a figure—if he really wanted to know how much it would take for her to agree to this crazy plan… 'All right, you asked—two hundred and fifty thousand dollars. That's my price.'

And his eyes might have damned her to hell and back, but he smiled—he actually smiled—and her stomach dropped to the floor like a brick even before he said his next word.

'Done.' He turned and yelled for Kareem. 'Prepare for the ceremony.'

Tora was reeling. 'But—'

'But nothing,' he said, smiling like the cat that had the cream. 'You named your price. I agreed. The deal is done.'

Kareem married them, neatly fitting the ceremony in between Tora feeding Atiyah her bottle and changing the infant's nappy, the bride's gown nothing more than black trousers and a fawn-coloured shirt with smudges of baby milk on the shoulder.

It wasn't a ceremony as such. There was nothing more to it than for the two of them to stand before Kareem in his white robes and with her hand on Rashid's, and for Kareem to utter a few words, before Rashid dropped his hand, jettisoning hers in the process, and saying, 'Right, that's that out of the way. Let's get this adoption signed off, shall we?'

Out of the way? thought Tora, feeling stunned as she returned to her seat and changed Atiyah. So that was it, then. No *You may kiss the bride.* No congratulations or champagne or even a pretence of celebration. She was married to Rashid, according to Qajarese law, and it felt—*hollow.*

Marriage wasn't supposed to feel hollow, she was sure. She'd always imagined getting married would be one of the happiest days of her life, with her father to walk her down the aisle and her mother proudly and no doubt tearfully looking on. Sure, that was before the glider accident that had killed them, but even now she would have liked to think of them somewhere up there looking down on her approvingly on her big day…

She gulped down on that bubble of disappointment before it could become something more.

This was hardly her big day though.

This was a means to an end for her, exactly as it was to him, the opportunity for her to obtain the funds she'd promised Sally, a formality in order for him to adopt Atiyah. After all, it wasn't as if she *wanted* to be married to Rashid, even if he made her feel like no more than an adjunct to the process, like a box that had been ticked or a task on a to-do list that had been crossed off.

He'd dropped her hand as if he couldn't bear to touch her. My God, what a difference, when last night he hadn't been able to stop touching her.

Then again, what had she expected? Last night might as well have been a lifetime ago. Rashid had been a different man—attentive, creative and infinitely attuned to her pleasure—and she'd been someone she didn't even recognise. Impulsive, reckless and brazen in bed. She'd behaved like a wanton.

She dragged in a breath, trying to find calm in a world that was teetering off balance. She'd shocked herself last night at just how shameless she'd been, as if the frustrations of Matt's betrayal and the despair of letting Sally and Steve down had spilled over on an effervescent tidal wave of passion that had washed away her moral values. Last night there'd been no off switch, no holding back. Talk about out of character for a girl who normally wouldn't kiss a guy until at least the second date.

Memories of that night should have been her secret thrill, something to smile privately about and wonder at her bravado and total abandonment. Not something to be constantly reminded of every minute of the day by being confronted with the star performer of her night of the pleasures of the flesh. The last thing she'd wanted was to learn that the man at the centre of her night of nights was Flight Nanny's and her very next client.

No, she wouldn't want her parents around to witness this. One day she'd marry for real. One day she'd find a man she loved and who loved her more than anything, and they'd be married under a brilliant blue sky and her parents could look down upon her and smile.

One day.

She slipped Atiyah's legs back into her sleep suit and did up the snaps. Think of the money, she told herself. Think of Sally and Steve and the quarter of a million dollars, merely for marrying Rashid for however long it took. Even if nothing else, now she'd have the money to complete this deal, without having to beg from the banks. Now there'd be nothing stopping Sally and Steve heading for Germany and the radical new treatment that might save him. Just as soon as she managed to give Rashid the bank account details for the transfer of the promised funds.

No wonder she felt a little hollowness in her gut.

The pilot came back then, smiling as he advised them personally they would be beginning their descent soon, and to assure them all would be well.

All would be well? She held Atiyah in her arms and softly sang her a favourite nursery rhyme, wanting to cuddle the baby for as long as she could before she'd have to be strapped into her capsule on the seat for landing.

After a night with Rashid and a mad on-paper marriage, she wasn't sure things would ever be well again.

It was done.

Kareem had completed the paperwork on both the marriage and then the adoption in short order.

His faux wife was installed and Atiyah was adopted and for now he could take a deep breath. That was one crisis averted.

His friends would laugh. Rashid married, just as they had warned him. Well, he would let them laugh. It wasn't as though it was a real marriage. It wasn't as though he was in love as Bahir and Kadar had attested to be, and it wasn't that he had to marry and impregnate a wife before he could be crowned Emir, as Zoltan had been required to do by the ancient texts of Al-Jirad when he had married the Princess Aisha.

He grunted. Though if that had been a requirement, he'd already well and truly ticked that box. Memories of last night's passion rolled through him like replays of a movie, except this was a movie in which he'd had a starring role. He'd only needed to touch her hand to be reminded of the satin smoothness of her skin, and to remember the sleek feminine beauty of the curve of her hip, the dip to the gentle round of her belly and all the places above and below that his fingers, and then his lips, had traversed.

He hadn't held her hand a second longer than he'd needed to, and yet the mere touch of her had fired his memories and kindled a need that burned like coals inside him.

There was too much going on in his life without complicating it with a woman that had blown his world apart.

He looked over his shoulder, through the gap in the seats, and saw her holding the child as if she were her own, the baby all dark-eyed innocence staring up at her as she spoke words he could not make out. What was with that? Atiyah was nothing to do with her.

So why did she seem to care so much?

Atiyah was supposed to be his sister, after all, even if the sister he'd never asked for or wanted.

And the wrongness of it all got to him and something inside him snapped.

He got out of his seat, determined to tell her so, but as he drew closer he realised she wasn't talking to the child, she was singing to it, some kind of lullaby, and she was looking down at the baby so intently, she didn't hear his approach.

He didn't interrupt at first—for a moment he couldn't because he was rooted to the spot—because for some reason he recognised the music. The notes were buried, but they were there and they were true, and each note she sang was like a shovel in his gut, exposing more.

'What are you singing?' he growled, when he could wait no longer, because he had to know.

Her singing stopped, and she looked up, suspicious, her eyes wide at finding him so close. 'Just a lullaby. I think it's Persian. Why?' she said, and suspicion turned to concern as she scanned his features. 'Is something wrong?'

He didn't know. All he knew was that there was something churning in his gut that brought him out in a cold sweat and made his skin crawl. How would he know the tune to a lullaby he was sure he'd never heard before?

But the way she was looking at him, as if he were mad, or worse… He looked for something that he could talk about to cover his confusion. His eyes fell on the infant. 'How is she?' he forced out, his mind clamouring to remember why he was here. 'I thought babies were supposed to scream through flights.'

Her doubting eyes told him she knew he hadn't come back to discuss the flying habits of babies. 'She's a good baby. Have you changed your mind? Would you like to hold her a while?'

He looked away, wondering where his anger had gone. He'd been sure he was angry when he'd left his seat, but now he was wondering why.

'Only I get the impression you haven't had a lot to do with babies. Do you have no other brothers or sisters?'

'No.'

'Babies aren't hard to look after,' she said. 'They just need to know they're loved.'

Well, that was the problem right there. How was he supposed to let a child know it was loved when he wasn't entirely sure how that was supposed to work? What did he have to offer? 'Look,' he said, 'I really just came back—to make sure you were comfortable.'

Liar.

She knew it, too, and yet still she attempted a smile. A nervous smile. She snagged her bottom lip between her teeth, before saying, 'Rashid, now that you're here, can I ask you something?'

'What?'

The 'fasten seat belt' sign lit up then and she put the baby back in her capsule, fastening the clasp over her belly and checking the seat belt. When she looked back up, her teeth were scraping over her bottom lip again. 'It's just about the money. I need to have it transferred as soon as possible.'

He breathed out on a sigh as resentment seeped like black ink into his mind, banishing his confusion with something he was entirely more comfortable with. 'The money.' He nodded. Now there was something that made sense. There was something he could understand. 'We haven't been married ten minutes and you can't wait to get your hands on your precious money.'

'Excuse me? You're the one who couldn't wait to land the plane before we were married. I've upheld my end of the bargain.'

'You expect the money now?'

'Well, we're married now, aren't we? So I thought—'

'You thought?' He was happy beyond measure that she'd turned the conversation away from where he felt so challenged and vulnerable and to money, which was solid and real and which he knew. 'You thought you could suddenly start dictating the terms?' Because if she thought that, then maybe it was time to start changing them.

'You're the one who agreed to pay me if I agreed to marry you.'

'Oh, you'll get your money, Ms Burgess. But I have to say, I'm disappointed you put so low a value on your services. I would have paid a million dollars, maybe even two for the pleasure of having you in my marital bed.'

Her face flushed bright red. 'Our deal didn't include me sleeping with you. I told you that wasn't going to happen.'

He was teasing her, of course. He had no intention of touching her again; he was still raw from losing himself too much—and too deeply—but her reaction pleased him inordinately and he was enjoying it. 'But you also told me you wouldn't marry me, and look at us now, happy newly-weds.'

'You can't make me sleep with you. That's unconscionable.'

He leaned down, one hand on the back of her seat, the other toying with a tendril of hair that had come loose from her bun.

'Don't you think it's a bit late to take the moral high ground? Who was it who picked me up in a bar? And after last night I know you're no shy, retiring virgin. Far from it. Why pretend you don't want a repeat of last night as much as I do?'

She swallowed and he tracked the movement in the kick of her chin and in her throat and his fingers let go of her hair to trail a line down the same way.

'I know what you think of me—that I'm cheap and easy.'

'I think you're expensive and easy, as it happens. But I'm willing to pay the price you ask.'

'Go to hell!'

'I have no doubt that's exactly where I'll end up. But don't fret, my charming wife, your reputation—or what's left of it—is safe with me. I have no intention of a repeat of last night's performance.'

CHAPTER EIGHT

QAJARAN CITY ROSE from the golden sands of the desert as if it had sprung from it organically, the buildings fashioned from bricks made of mud, hay and the desert sand itself, so their walls sparkled in places when the light caught on the tiny crystals as they passed, but it was the people that most fascinated Tora.

From the airport the streets were lined with people waving flags and clapping their hands—happy, smiling people. A woman in colourful robes held her young child aloft to better watch them pass, a crumpled old man leaning on walking sticks had tears running down his leathery cheeks but a smile so wide it was obvious they were tears of joy. And it struck her then that this was for Rashid—the man who might soon be their Emir, ruler of Qajaran—the man who was her new husband.

The same man whom she'd spent an illicit night of sex with.

The man who had barely an hour ago assured her there would be no repeat performance.

She trembled, the muscles between her thighs clamping down on a sudden bloom of heat in spite of his assurances. It was crazy, she should be exhausted after a night of little sleep and the drag of international flight halfway around the world, even if it was in the sumptuous surroundings of a private jet, but, looking across at Rashid, never had she felt more alive, never had she felt more aware of her sexuality.

Should she believe him when he said that it wouldn't happen again? Or was it just that she didn't want to?

Oh, God, it would be so much easier if she could simply hate him. He'd railroaded her into this deal, after all. Not without her agreement, but he'd done his best to make her feel small and mercenary even with that.

But…there was still that night between them—that unimaginable night of pleasure—how could she hate a man for that? And there were those moments since then when the blustering faltered and he looked lost and lonely and so achingly sad that she wanted to reach out to him. Because who couldn't love a tiny child? What had gone wrong in his life that he felt that he couldn't?

She wished she could hate him. Then she wouldn't be drawn to him. Then she wouldn't feel this damnable pull.

He'd told her there would be no repeat performance, but, when it came down to it, if he turned to her in the night she doubted whether she'd have the strength to say no to him. When she remembered back to the night they'd spent together and the masterful man he was then and all the ways he had pleasured her, it was hard to imagine why she'd even want to.

She looked out of the window at the people lining the street, all so keen for a glimpse of this man who might rule them, feeling shallow and superficial and hating herself right now. There was history being made here today and, even in her unsubstantial way, she was part of it, yet all she could think about was sex.

Well, that was Rashid's fault, too. That night they'd spent in each other's arms had a lot to answer for.

'Did you arrange this welcome committee?' she heard Rashid ask Kareem, and Tora looked at him, because his voice sounded as tight as his jaw looked, and as uncomfortable as it must feel. And for the first time, she saw Rashid looking like a man who was uncertain with his place in the world, and she was intrigued. He didn't seem like a man who would doubt himself.

'Good news has a way of getting out,' Kareem answered, with a shrug of his white-robed shoulders. 'Even in Qajaran, where the Internet is not as readily accessible as it is in the west. The people have waited a long time to see the

Qajarese flag flying on a royal limousine. Your return is welcome.'

'If I am to do this,' Rashid said, 'I am going to need help,' and if Tora wasn't mistaken there was a sheen of sweat on his forehead in this very much air-conditioned car.

Kareem smiled even as he bowed his head, as if Rashid had said exactly what he'd wanted him to. 'I am at your disposal, of course.'

'Thank you,' Rashid acknowledged. 'And I have a friend who had to lead his country unexpectedly. I would like to seek his advice.'

'You refer to Sheikh Zoltan, the King of Al-Jirad.'

'Yes. You know him?'

'But of course. Al-Jirad and Qajaran have been friends since ancient times. He would be most welcome here. It would further cement the bonds between our two countries.'

Rashid seemed to relax then, taking a deep breath and lifting his hand in acknowledgment as they passed the cheering onlookers. He looked the other way and caught Tora watching him as his gaze drifted past hers. His eyes immediately snapped back. 'What?'

'Nothing,' she said, shaking her head, for the first time feeling a little sorry for this man, who appeared to have been thrust into a world not of his making. Nothing she could tell him or that he would want to hear at any rate.

The limousine slowed as it waited for a set of high metal gates, sculpted to look like twin peacocks, to be opened. 'I have taken the liberty of installing you in the Old Palace,' Kareem said as they started along a long palm-lined driveway. 'Emir Malik built six new palaces during his reign, all of which are more modern, and you are more than welcome to make one of the others your base, but, for your comfort and the sake of tradition, I feel the Old Palace will be more suitable.'

Tora swallowed as she caught glimpses of a building out of her window through the garden of palms and greenery, the curve of a domed roof here, a peep of a decorative window arch there, snippets that held the promise of fantasy.

But of course, they would be heading for a palace. Where else would an Emir live?

And then the palms parted and the car rolled slowly past a fountain that was the size of a small lake, featuring stallions made of gleaming marble and standing tall on their hind legs, their manes alive to an unfelt breeze as they pranced in the tumbling water that sparkled like jewels in the sun.

But while the fountain was spectacular, it was

a mere accessory to the palace. Tora took one look and knew she'd left her old world behind and stepped into the pages of a fairy tale. Surely it was the most beautiful building she'd ever seen, with decorative arches and rows of columns and a golden dome adorning the roof, and the whole effect was as romantic as it was impressive.

The limousine rolled to a stop under a colonnaded entrance shaded from the weather and before a flight of stairs where a dozen uniformed men, wearing the colours of the flags she'd seen waved in the streets, stood waiting.

'Welcome home, Excellency, Sheikha,' Kareem said with a nod as one of the guards stepped forward to open the door.

Sheikha? Tora swallowed as she unfastened Atiyah's capsule and prepared to enter this strange new world. But of course, she supposed, she must be a sheikha if she was married to a sheikh.

And then she caught a glance of Rashid's grimly set jaw. She was married to this man. As good as shackled to the sheikh. *A fairy tale?* And suddenly Tora wasn't so sure.

'If you please, Sheikha Victoria,' Kareem said with a bow as he gestured her to enter, 'this is your suite.'

Tora was reeling. She'd thought the outside

of the palace was breathtaking, but then she'd stepped inside into air scented with jasmine and musk and known she was in some kind of fantasy land. Walls were decorated in gilt and mosaic, chairs and tables inlaid with mother of pearl. It was a feast for the eyes, and everywhere she looked another work of art demanded her attention. It was all she could do not to gape.

It was all she could do not to run. Still dressed in her serviceable, travel-weary uniform while everything around her was exotic and beautiful, she had never felt more out of place.

And now Kareem was showing them a suite that would swallow up her entire house in Sydney and still leave enough room to live in, and that was without taking into account the terrace overlooking the pool and garden outside her windows where the now setting sun was bathing everything including a row of mountains far in the distance in a ruby glow. It was utterly magical, and that was only the outside.

The bedroom itself was enormous, hosting a magnificent gilt four-poster bed, and there was a room prepared for Atiyah along with another room for Yousra, a local girl who'd been assigned to be her nursery maid, and the main bathroom had a bath that put some of the lap pools at home to shame.

Her suite. All hers. Which meant that Rashid

would be sleeping elsewhere, and for the first time since arriving Tora started to relax. If she wanted to avoid Rashid, she need never leave the safety of her room.

She eyed the four-poster bed longingly. Weary from both the travel and the emotional roller coaster of the last however many hours since she'd walked into her cousin's office, already she imagined herself lost in blissful sleep amongst the cushions and the pillows. Tomorrow would be soon enough to chase up the funds Rashid had promised and let Sally know they were coming. By then she might be able to sound convincing when she told Sally that her delay in returning home was caused by nothing more than a simple request to stay while Atiyah settled in. Not that anyone was likely to believe her if she did tell them the truth.

But that could wait until tomorrow. Once Tora had bathed and fed Atiyah and seen her comfortable, bed was the first place she was headed.

'And through this door,' Kareem continued, opening a door of exquisitely carved timber, 'is Your Excellency's suite. The rooms are interconnecting, of course.'

'But of course,' said Rashid with a smirk in Tora's direction.

He was teasing her again, she realised. No more than taunting her. And yet all of a sudden

Tora's sprawling apartment didn't seem anywhere near big enough.

Atiyah cried out, growing restless, and Tora saw her chance.

'If that is all?' she asked, not interested in venturing into Rashid's apartments. 'I will take care of Atiyah. She's had a long day.'

'Cannot Yousra take care of the child for you?' Kareem asked. 'Would you not like to dine together with us?'

While the girl's eyes looked up at her hopefully, Rashid's dark eyes gleamed, his lips turned up in one corner. He knew she was avoiding him and right now she didn't care.

'I will welcome Yousra's assistance, of course,' Tora said, smiling at the girl so as not to offend her, but also because she really would appreciate the help, especially when sleep tugged so hard at her, 'but Atiyah has been through many changes recently, and until she's settled in I'd like to keep some routine in her life. Besides, I'm sure you and Rashid have many matters to discuss that don't require my input.'

'As you wish,' Kareem said with a bow, and Tora was surprised to see what looked like approval in his eyes. 'I will have your meal sent up.' He touched his fingers to Atiyah's brow, uttered a blessing to the child and wished Tora goodnight.

'I'll see you later,' said Rashid.

'Seven in the morning for breakfast?' Tora suggested, refusing to acknowledge the implicit threat in his words. 'That would be perfect. We have some details to discuss also. Goodnight.'

And the flash of his eyes and the flare of his nostrils told her he did not like her dictating when they would meet or being so summarily dismissed. No doubt, he didn't like being reminded about his end of the bargain either. Tough. He had promised, he could pay up. 'Come,' said Tora, turning to Yousra. 'Let's give Atiyah her bath now.'

With a swish of Kareem's robes, she heard him disappear with Rashid through the interconnecting door and Tora could breathe again.

Zoltan was coming. Rashid felt the tight bunching ache in his gut loosen a fraction, but it was fraction enough to be able to breathe more deeply than he had since arriving in Qajaran. He gazed out from his terrace over the gardens surrounding the expansive pool below. Around him the palace slept. Night had fallen fast and now the sky above was a velvet shroud of blue black.

Zoltan would arrive in three days, to be joined by Aisha and the children, and Bahir and Kadar with their own families, the day before the coronation. The last time they had been together had been in Melbourne for Kadar's wedding six months ago. It would be good for the desert brothers to be together again, although once there were just four of them, and now every time they got together there seemed to be more, wives and children swelling their numbers. He shook his head. Such an eventuality would have been unthinkable even a few years ago, one by one his brothers falling into marriage.

He alone was left. He wasn't counting his hastily contrived marriage to Tora. It wasn't as if she were a real wife. She would be gone in a matter of weeks, even if their marriage needed to last a year on paper. In some ways, it was unfortunate that his desert brothers and their wives would meet her at all, for they were bound to make something of this temporary arrangement.

He heard a sound and looked sideways towards where Tora's suite of apartments lay, but the night settled into quiet again, the rustle of the palm fronds on the barely there breeze the only sound.

He sighed. Well, let his brothers make of it what they would. He had much more important things to think about now, like a country full of people who had been offered morsels through years where the Emir had grown rich on its resource revenues. Things needed to change. Less money would be lavished on palaces and fripperies. More money would go to funding schools and hospitals, especially outside the city, where needs went unseen and often ignored when they were.

His grip on the alabaster balustrade of the balcony tightened until his knuckles hurt.

It was easy to see where the inequities and injustices lay, but there was so much to address. Could he fix the problems of the past thirty years of maladministration?

Why was he even considering it?

But then somebody had to do it—share the riches and drag this country into the twenty-first century—and he was next in line to the throne.

His gut screwed tighter all over again. God, what was he even doing here? He was a petroleum engineer by day with a reputation as a playboy by night. Apart from his DNA, what qualifications did he have to equip him to run a country?

He looked around. There was that sound again. The child, he realised. But this time there was more.

She was singing that song again.

Both drawn and repelled in the same instant, he watched as Tora emerged from her suite, the baby clutched in her arms as she sang the soft, soothing words of a lullaby he never knew and yet that somehow tugged at some deep part of him. He melted into the shadows as she swayed in the night air, singing words of comfort and peace, her hair down out of that damned bun, just the way he liked it, while the blue light from the pool below turned her long white nightdress translucent so that it floated like a cloud around her slim legs and tickled the tops of her bare feet.

He swallowed back on a surge of lust as he watched, transfixed.

The breeze toyed with the hem of her night-dress, shifting shadows and whispering promises as she sang of apricots and pigeons and waterfalls, and some of her words were wrong or mispronounced, but it didn't matter because the overall effect was still beautiful.

She was beautiful.

He stood in the shadows with his heart beating too fast at a mystery he didn't understand.

He stood there utterly bewitched.

Bewitched and rock hard.

She finished the song, the last of the sweet notes trailing away on the night air, the baby in her arms asleep. She turned to go back inside the same moment as he emerged from the shadows. She gasped.

'Tora.'

And she took a deep breath and then another. 'You frightened me. What are you doing on my terrace?'

He looked back the way he had come. 'It appears we have adjoining terraces, as well as adjoining suites.'

Her eyes blinked her disappointment before shuttering down. 'Well, goodnight.'

'Tora, wait.'

'Why? Atiyah needs to go back to bed.'

He looked at the child, her face at peace in Tora's arms, oblivious to the electricity charging the air between them. 'She's asleep.'

'Which is where I want to be.'

'Tora.'

'Why are you here?'

'I couldn't sleep.'

'No,' she said, her soft voice tremulous in the velvet night, 'why are you *here*? What do you want?'

A heartbeat later he answered. 'You.' And in that moment, Tora lost all perception of time, all cognizance of space. Because Rashid was standing there in nothing more than thin white sleep pants slung low over his hips that made no secret of his arousal. And his chest was bare and in his eyes she could see torment and right now he looked as if he'd been sculpted in shadow.

And then he drew closer and she could see there was more than torment in his dark eyes—something far more carnal.

She shuddered from the top of her head all the way to the tips of toes that curled on the cool paving stone, seeking to get a grip on a world where she was a stranger.

'Rashid...' But he was already stepping closer, stepping into her space even as she drew back, her arms protecting the baby, leaving her defenceless as his fingers laced through her hair.

'Rashid...'

And then his lips brushed hers and she breathed him in and he tasted warm and musky and male and his taste and scent sent her spinning back to the place she'd been that first night. *So good.* So very good that her body hummed into life as readily as if his lips had flicked a switch.

Oh, God.

She wasn't about to turn it off.

His lips were as soft as the night sky, the sweep of his tongue like a shooting star to her senses, and there was magic in the air all around them.

Instinctively she opened to him—she knew him—and his kiss deepened. Hardened. As he angled his head and pulled her closer.

There was a squawk. A protest from between them. And Tora's attention snapped back to the child in her arms—to where it should have been before she'd been seduced by the shadows. She turned her face away, freeing a hand to push at the hard wall of his naked chest.

'Rashid, stop.'

He blinked, feeling sideswiped all over again. This woman did things to him. She made him forget himself and his determination to lock down his emotions when he was around her. She made him forget everything. He'd been so blind-sided by lust that he'd forgotten completely about the child in her arms—his own tiny sister. And he'd known all along that he would be rubbish caring for an infant, and still he felt ashamed.

'Is…is she all right?'

'She's fine,' Tora said, rocking her in her arms. 'No harm done.' Although the quake in her voice told him otherwise. 'Maybe you should go back to your suite.'

He reached out for her. He didn't want to go. 'Tora—' but she spun away.

'Stop it! Don't you care about this baby at all?'

'I adopted her, didn't I?'

'Lucky Atiyah.'

'Look,' he said, shaking his head as he turned it towards the heavens, 'I didn't ask to take on the care of an infant. I don't know the first thing about babies.'

'Well, maybe you should start learning because frankly, Atiyah deserves better. You have a ten-week-old child who has lost her parents and you treat her like something you wished you could shove away in a filing cabinet somewhere and forget about.

'Don't you understand? She's not a thing, Rashid, she's a child. A baby. She needs to be nurtured, not merely tolerated. She needs love and smiles and someone who truly cares about her. Instead, she got stuck with you—sullen, resentful, miserable you—and I can't work out why you have to be that way. Have you forgotten what it's like to be a child?'

His jaw was so tightly clenched, he felt a muscle pop. 'No, as a matter of fact I haven't, but rest assured I don't plan on sending Atiyah to boarding school to be looked after by strangers the first chance I get, so I guess I do know something about bringing up children, even if it's nowhere near your high standards. But thanks anyway, for pointing out my failings so succinctly.' He turned to leave and this time it was her that stopped him.

'Rashid,' she said, concern swirling in her gentle eyes. 'Is that what happened to you? How old were you when they sent you away?'

'It doesn't matter,' he said on a sigh, raking a hand through his hair. 'Other than the fact it makes me the most useless person ever to be appointed guardian of anyone, let alone an infant like Atiyah.' He looked down at the baby, now settled again. 'She deserves better.' He turned his eyes up to Tora's. 'I'm sorry I interrupted you. Goodnight,' he said, and he was gone.

Tora stepped breathlessly back into her suite, meeting a distraught-looking Yousra coming the other way. 'Is everything all right? I heard voices,' she said as she caught sight of the child in Tora's arms. 'Oh, no. I should have woken. Did she cry? I am so sorry not to let you sleep.'

'It's okay,' Tora soothed her. 'I would normally be awake at this time and I was only half asleep. You go back to bed.'

And the younger woman bowed. 'If it pleases you, Sheikha.'

'Call me Tora,' she said. 'I am much more comfortable with that.'

'But...?'

'Tora,' she insisted. 'As I call you Yousra. We are both looking after Atiyah after all. We should be friends.'

The young girl smiled uncertainly and bowed some more. 'If you are sure, Sheikha,' and Tora smiled as the young woman withdrew.

Tora settled Atiyah back into her bed and watched her for a while, marvelling at how placid she was in the wake of having had her world turned upside down, a world that at ten weeks she'd only just been getting to grips with. Tora ran one fingertip across her downy cheek. She was a little sweetheart, no two ways about it.

A sweetheart with a tortured brother. What had happened that he felt so incapable of loving Atiyah? What kind of childhood had he had? Boarding school, and from an early age by the sounds. But why, when his father had only recently died? Why would he have done that?

She crawled back into her bed, and tucked her knees up under her crossed arms, trying not to think about how in Sydney it would be halfway through the afternoon instead halfway through the night, trying not to think about the meeting with Rashid at breakfast that she had asked for and that now seemed so close as the clock edged closer to a Qajarese morning.

Thinking instead of how she could help him overcome whatever failings he thought he had and bond with his tiny sister.

Thinking that she cared because she wanted Atiyah to be happy.

She stretched her legs out and laid her head back in her deep, welcoming pillows. It was nothing to do with the ache she could feel in Rashid's eyes. All she wanted was for Atiyah to be happy.

That was all.

CHAPTER NINE

THE SOFT SKY outside her windows was layered in pink and blue like cotton candy when Tora rose. Atiyah was gurgling and examining her hands and fingers when Tora peeked over the side of her cot.

'Good morning, beautiful,' she said, only to be rewarded by a big, gummy smile that made her heart sing. 'Oh, you sweetheart,' she said, lifting her up as Yousra appeared with a tray of coffee.

'She's awake?' asked the girl.

'Yes, and she's smiling. Look,' and Yousra came closer and tickled her tummy and the baby kicked her little legs and made a sound like a hiccup and both women laughed.

They played with her until it was almost time for Tora's meeting with Rashid. There were preparations being made outside on the terrace—she could hear someone giving instructions as staff set a table for two. Breakfast on the terrace overlooking the pool? That should be pleasant enough, if only it didn't remind her of what had happened on that terrace last night.

She closed her eyes as she twisted her hair into

a bun and pinned it to her head, trying to keep her mind on how she was going to get Rashid and Atiyah together and not thinking about that kiss. She really would have to keep her distance, especially when the velvet shadows of the night stroked her soul and dimmed her logic. No more night-time wandering for her. No more assuming she was alone.

And definitely no more kissing. She touched a finger to her lips, wondering how a man who could be so hard and cold could feel so gentle and warm…

She shook her head to banish the thought. Oh, no. She wouldn't go making that mistake again. If she hadn't been holding Atiyah, she didn't know how it might have ended.

Liar. She knew exactly how.

On her back.

Or in the shower.

No! She could not afford to think of that night in Sydney. That was in the past, when they had been nothing more than strangers in the night. Things were different now. She had a job to do and she would show him that he could not just click his fingers to get his way. If she achieved nothing else before she left, she would show him that he could love Atiyah.

She gave her hair and make-up a final check before adding a slick of neutral lip gloss. There, cool and professional on the outside at least, just the way she needed to be for this meeting. She wouldn't let him rattle her today. Besides, she was too happy to be rattled. Because Atiyah had smiled.

Rashid was already seated at the table reading some papers when she approached. The sun was still low enough not to cause them any grief, but there was the promise of heat in the air. He glanced up disapprovingly. 'Haven't you got anything else to wear?'

Tora sighed as she sat down. If she'd thought that his opening up to her a little last night might have made his attitude towards her less adversarial, she was wrong. The walls between them were up again, not that she was about to let him spoil her good mood. 'Good morning to you, too. I trust you slept well.'

He grunted as a waiter appeared, laying a napkin across her lap and fetching a dish with yoghurt and fruit before enquiring if she'd like tea or coffee. She smiled and asked for coffee, waiting for it to be poured while all the time she was aware of the man opposite simmering where he sat.

'It's a beautiful morning,' she said, when the waiter had departed.

'You can't expect to wear—' he nodded disdainfully in the direction of her clothes, ignoring what she'd said '—*that* every day.'

Tora looked down at her clothes, at her short-sleeved shirt and skirt, both fresh and, as far as she knew it, baby-spew free. 'What's wrong with what I'm wearing?'

'Nothing, if you've got a thing about those boring shirts you probably call a uniform. For the record, I don't.'

'*You're* wearing a shirt.' Although, to be fair, it was one hell of a lot sexier than hers, the white cotton so fine she could see his skin tone and the darker circles of his areolae where the fabric skimmed his chest. *Damn.* She looked away and concentrated on her coffee.

'Couldn't you find something more appropriate?'

'It's a funny thing,' she said with a smile, refusing to be pulled into Rashid's dark cloud of a mood, 'but, for some strange reason, I seem to have left all my resort wear at home. Go figure.' She shrugged. 'Besides I actually like my uniform. It's comfortable, practical and it scares men away—well, it usually scares men away… present company excepted, of course.' Her friend Sally had always joked that she'd worn her uniform as a form of self-defence against unwanted attention, and she wasn't right exactly, but it generally didn't bring Tora too much interest from the opposite sex. 'Men aren't supposed to like bookish-looking women. Come to think of it, did you miss that memo?'

He scowled. 'What's got you so cheerful?'

'You mean aside from seeing you?' she said, smirking as she sipped her coffee, savouring the heady aroma of the spiced brew, before she continued, 'Red letter day. Atiyah smiled this morning. Maybe you should try taking a leaf out of her book some time.'

'She smiled,' he said, frowning a little. 'Is that good?'

'It's better than good, it's great. It's the first smile I've seen her give. You want her to be happy, don't you?'

'Of course,' he said, with as much conviction as if the concept had never occurred to him. And then he nodded and his eyes softened. 'Of course, yes, I want her to be happy.'

'There you go,' she said, feeling that he was not the lost cause he made out and that he would overcome whatever was holding him back from embracing his new role. 'I swear, you won't be able to resist falling in love with her when she smiles at you. I wish I'd brought her now, so you could see for yourself.'

He looked at a loss for what to say next, as if once again he was in unfamiliar territory. 'Anyway,' he said, 'you're supposed to be the wife of the Emir. You can't wear that every day—you'd look ridiculous. Kareem told me last night he'd organised an entire wardrobe of clothes for you.'

'Oh.' Is that what that was about? She'd opened the door to the walk-in wardrobe last night wondering where she could stash her suitcase and found it bursting at the seams with garments. Robes of silk and the finest cottons and in all the colours of the rainbow. And she'd shut the door again because they obviously weren't hers and found another place to leave her case. She picked up her spoon to try her yoghurt.

Rashid glanced at his watch. 'What did you want to talk to me about?'

Right. She put her spoon down again. Clearly this wasn't a breakfast meeting where one actually expected to eat breakfast. In spite of her good mood, her heart gave a little trip at having to broach the subject again. But there was no point beating about the bush. She pulled a folded paper from her pocket. 'Here are the bank details for you to transfer the funds.'

He took it, checking the details before his eyes flicked back to hers. 'Not your account?'

'It's a trust account for a firm of solicitors.' *Matt's solicitors*, she thought, biting her lip. Damn. She really wanted nothing to do with Matt or his cronies, but it would just have to do for now.

'A trust account?' His eyebrows raised, he cast his eyes over her shirt again. 'You know, you're much more interesting that that uniform lets on. But then, we already knew that.' He put the paper down on his others. 'So, was there anything else?'

'You'll do it?' she said, hardly believing it would be that simple after the grief he'd given her on the plane. 'Today?'

His eyes narrowed, as if they were trying to find a way inside her to gain the answers he wanted, but still he said, 'It will be done today. Was that all?'

'Not quite,' she said. 'There is one more thing. I'd like Internet access. I see it's password protected.'

'You wish to Tweet that you're now sheikha of Qajaran?'

She grimaced. 'Hardly. I need to contact my work and let them know there'll be a delay in me getting home so they can start reallocating assignments.' *And tell Sally the funds are on their way.* But he didn't need to know that.

'I'll have Kareem arrange it. Just be careful what you send from the palace.'

'Of course, I will.'

'Then,' he said, collecting his papers as he rose to his feet, 'if there's nothing more, I'll leave you to it. Enjoy your breakfast.'

* * *

Rashid had indigestion but it had nothing to do with what he'd eaten. He strode through the palace towards the library he'd chosen last night with Kareem for his office, his stomach complaining the entire way. Cursing Tora the entire way.

Because he still had to make the biggest decision of his life and, with her around, he couldn't think straight.

And it didn't seem to matter how much he tried to block her out and tell himself that she was irrelevant, she was there, alternately smiling, needling or offering him sympathy.

He shook his head as he walked down the long passageways. Why had he told her what he had last night? His past was his business, nobody else's. It was not the kind of thing he shared with anyone, let alone a woman he'd picked up in a bar.

But then, that was not all she was. Tora was much more than a casual pick-up.

She was his sister's carer.

And now she was his wife, even if in name only.

And he wanted her despite all his claims and words to the contrary, wanted her like there was no tomorrow. Last night was proof enough of that. He'd been blind with desire and she'd come willingly into his kiss, only stopping when Atiyah had protested.

He'd beaten himself up at the time, thinking he was the one at fault, but when he'd thought about it much later, in the long hours when sleep had eluded him, he'd realised that she'd made no effort to push him away before Atiyah had cried—she'd been as much a participant in that kiss as he had been—which proved to him that he wasn't the only one feeling this way. Feeling this need.

It wasn't just one-sided. There was still unfinished business between them.

So why was he fighting it? What point was there to erecting walls between them, when they seemed so futile and no wall had yet stopped him from wanting her?

Maybe it would be better to deal with the problem head-on, rather than pretending it didn't exist. Sleep with her. Get it out of his system so he could at least think straight.

He needed to think straight.

He paused, his hands on the door to the library.

Then again, maybe he was better off keeping his distance. She was trouble. Madonna, siren and shrew all wrapped up in one irritating package.

He snorted. Yeah, he'd tried leaving her alone and look how far that had got him. But he could hardly just tell her he'd changed his mind about his hands-off policy and expect her to go for it. She'd made it plain she wasn't about to simply fall into bed with him again at a click of his fingers. But what to do?

Fed up with torturing himself over her, he pulled open the doors.

'Excellency,' said Kareem, who was waiting for him inside, already busy at his notes and making his countless plans for Rashid while he waited. 'I trust you slept well.'

'More or less,' he said, not wanting to think about how little he'd slept or any more about the why. 'So what do we have to consider today?'

'Many things,' Kareem confirmed. 'But I know it is all very dry and Sheikh Zoltan will be here soon so I thought perhaps tomorrow we might take a tour of Malik's new palaces, to see if you would prefer to use one of them for your official residence.'

'If you think it's important. How many were there again?'

'Six.'

Good grief. Rashid suppressed a sigh, feeling already weighed down with the volume of the historical and economic texts he had been given to digest. 'Are there not more important matters to consider?'

'Certainly. But if I can use an expression you might well know, Rome wasn't built in a day.

You arc yet to accept this role, and anyone would be foolish to expect you to conquer it overnight. There are things to be assessed in the kingdom that do not require your poring through old documents or dusty tomes twenty-four hours a day, things that might give you a broader view of the kingdom, before your possible coronation.'

'Fine,' Rashid conceded, pinching the bridge of his nose with his fingers. 'Arrange it.'

Kareem bowed. 'It will be done.'

And suddenly Rashid had a brainwave. 'What about Tora? Could she come, too?'

'Sheikha Victoria?' The vizier shook his head while he deliberated. 'I don't see why not. She would no doubt appreciate seeing some more of our architecture.'

'So long as it won't cause any problems, if people were to see Tora with me, only for her to subsequently disappear?'

Kareem looked unabashed as he weighed the air with his big hands. 'This will not be a problem. In past years, our people are used to seeing our Emir with any one of a number of consorts, and frankly they would be more surprised to think you were unmarried.'

'Excellent,' said Rashid, rubbing his hands together as he found his first smile for the day. Maybe a day out with him would prove to her he was not the sullen, resentful and miserable monster she had painted him. Maybe if they could be friends first, they could be more… 'Now, where were we?'

Tora was enjoying a day of sheer girly fun. It started in the morning, with Yousra giving her a tour of the various gardens of the palace and around the pools and fountains where the lush foliage and flowers and sprays of water combined to turn the air deliciously cool and fragrant while tiny birds darted from bush to bush. It was exotic and different and serene. And after her tense breakfast with Rashid, Tora felt that serenity seep into her bones and she could breathe again.

Just when she thought it couldn't get any better or more beautiful, Yousra showed her to the secret garden, hidden away in a courtyard and thick with trees and palms that gave way to a lily pond where small ducklings paddled. And there tucked away in the centre like a gift-wrapped jewel stood a square pavilion with ivory-coloured columns and red balustrade with a tiled roof and white curtains for walls that billowed gently from on high.

'It's beautiful,' she said, cursing the inadequacy of the description as Yousra smiled, waiting for her reaction. It was like something from a fairy tale that became more so as two peacocks emerged from the foliage and quietly wandered away. Tora was entranced by it all. 'What is it?'

'It is called the Pavilion of Mahabbah and was built by Emir Haalim when his favourite wife died. This was her favourite courtyard, you see. And he had loved her so much he had named her after the Qajarese word for love—*mahabbah*. It is said he filled this pool with his tears. Come,' she said, leading the way. 'I have arranged us to take tea there.'

'So it is the pavilion of love,' Tora said a few minutes later as she sat on one of the low sofas, thinking how appropriate it was, how romantic and how tragic, imagining the Emir standing between the curtains, looking out over the pond and remembering his beloved wife. Beside her on the rug on the floor, Atiyah played under a baby gym, kicking her legs as she swatted at the hanging toys above her with her little hands. 'He must have really loved her.'

Yousra nodded. 'The heart of a Qajarese Emir is worth the hearts of ten men. And it is said the Emir loves ten times truer.'

Tora sipped her tea, not wanting to argue, but not entirely sure that was true for all the Emirs. Malik might have loved ten times as many as other men with his palaces full of harems, and then there was Rashid.

She wanted to believe Rashid had a heart. She

hadn't seen much evidence of it so far, but she so wanted it to be there, if only so his sister might grow up surrounded by love rather than indifference. And she wondered again about a man who'd let slip that his own childhood had been lacking. Something dreadful had happened to him, that much was clear, something bound up in a tortured history that had scarred him deeply and, if she wasn't mistaken, was still hurting.

She shouldn't care, she told herself. He was nothing to her but the means to fund a promise she'd made to her best friend. Nothing more to her than that—if she discounted one heated night of the best sex she'd ever had and one stolen kiss last night that she hadn't wanted to end.

She really shouldn't care.

And yet it was hard not to.

The afternoon provided a different kind of entertainment. There were just the three of them, Tora, Yousra and Atiyah, amidst a dressing room overflowing with the most amazing clothes Tora had ever seen.

Yousra sat holding Atiyah on the sofa at the end of the four-poster bed, as Tora turned model and tried on garment after garment to much applause and encouragement in between cups of honey tea and sweets made of nuts and dried figs, apricots and dates. Yousra advised her on which were more suitable for during the day, and which she might consider for night-time events like formal dinners.

How Kareem had pulled this off, Tora wondered as she slipped into another gown, she had no idea. They'd all been on their way to Qajaran when this whole mad marriage scheme had been contrived, so he would have had to have messaged ahead from the plane with his instructions.

Clearly it was a different world when one was connected to royalty.

'That one, yes!' said Yousra, as Tora turned to the young woman wearing a robe of aqua-coloured silk, embroidered around the neckline and the cuffs of the sleeves. 'That colour suits you so well. You look beautiful.'

Tora turned to the mirror and was inclined to agree. But then it was a beautiful gown, whisper-soft against her skin and so cool. 'I like it,' she said, and moved on to the next.

And after she'd exhausted both the contents of the wardrobe and tiny Atiyah, who'd been put down for a nap, Tora couldn't bear to go back to her serviceable skirt and shirt, but returned to the aqua gown that felt so deliciously cool against her skin. Yousra brushed out her hair and made up her eyes, so she had Qajaran eyes, she called them, ringed with kohl, before she hennaed Tora's feet. 'Just a little,' she said, 'for you will have your hands and feet done for the coronation.' Tora returned the favour by painting Yousra's fingernails and toenails and making the younger woman giggle as she tickled her toes.

They were both laughing as they compared the results when there was a knock on the door and Rashid entered.

'Nice to see someone having fun,' he said, his eyes sweeping the room to take in the situation. 'Won't all that noise wake the baby?'

Yousra bowed immediately, her hands clasped demurely in her lap, her painted toes tucked discreetly under her robe, as if she'd been chastised. 'Excuse me,' she said softly.

Tora saw no reason for repentance. She did see an opportunity for bringing Rashid closer towards caring for his sister. 'It's actually a fallacy babies need silence to sleep. They hear plenty of noise while in the womb and it is good for a child to grow up hearing laughter. Come and see for yourself how untroubled she is.'

His eyes raked over her. Confused eyes, as if he didn't know how to respond, so she slipped her hand in his and steered him towards Atiyah's darkened room, pulling aside the netting. Atiyah lay on her back, one hand to the side of her head as she slept. 'You see,' she said with a smile as she looked up at him. 'Sleeping like a baby. Isn't she beautiful?'

He supposed she was, with her black curls framing her face and her eyes a dark line of lashes, her lips pink and perfectly serene. He nodded. 'She is,' and only then, when he went to reach out a hand to see if the skin of her cheek was as smooth as it looked, realised Tora's hand was still in his. 'I take your point,' he said, and squeezed her fingers before he let them go, and touched fingers warmed by Tora's to his sister's cheek. So smooth. So perfect. The baby stirred slightly before sighing back into sleep, and Rashid took his hand away so he didn't disturb her more.

Tora was still smiling and it was all he could do not to pull her into his arms, but no, that was not the way. 'Kareem gave me this for you,' he said, pulling a paper from between the books he carried, and handed her the instructions for accessing the Internet.

'Thank you,' she said.

'And your money has been transferred.'

Tora closed her eyes and clutched the paper to her chest. 'Thank you so much for letting me know.'

She looked beautiful. She'd ditched the drab uniform and that too-tight bun and was wearing a silken robe that didn't cling and yet that turned her into a woman again, the woman he knew was hidden below, with breasts and hips and curves in between, and she'd done something with her eyes so they looked smoky and seductive and now, because of something he'd said, she looked radiant.

He'd been mad to ever imagine he could leave her alone.

'There's more,' he said, and his voice sounded thick even to him. 'Kareem is giving me a tour of the six new palaces tomorrow, and I came to ask you if you would like to accompany me.'

'Me?'

Her eyes had lit up, as if she wanted to say yes, but they were wary. Guarded. She didn't trust him. She had good cause. 'You.'

She looked down at the child. 'And Atiyah?'

'There is no reason to haul her around with us. We will be in and out of cars in the heat of the day. She will be much more comfortable staying here.'

'But—'

'Please, Sheikha, I can look after her.'

Tora looked at Yousra. 'Are you sure? We may be gone a long time by the sounds.'

'It is no trouble. Atiyah is a delight.'

'So, it's settled, then,' Rashid said, feeling better than he had in a long time. 'We will leave after breakfast.'

Tora looked up at him, her accentuated eyes hauntingly beautiful and her lips slightly parted. 'After breakfast, then,' she said as they walked towards the door.

But he turned back before leaving, wanting one more look at her, like this, like a woman dressed in silk and not a buttoned-up nursemaid with a bun. 'I see you found something else to wear.'

'Yes. You were right—Kareem had organised an entire wardrobe of clothes for me. Yousra's been helping me go through them.'

'I like what you're wearing,' he said, nodding at her choice. 'You look beautiful.'

And her lips moved uncertainly, but he didn't hear if she actually said anything, because he was gone.

CHAPTER TEN

THERE WERE SIX of them in all. A white palace, covered in mother of pearl shell that dazzled in the sun. A red palace with red turrets and domes that paid homage to the ruby. A palace with extensive scented gardens and called Yasmin—named after Malik's favourite of the time, they were informed—the Grand Palace that was based on a Venetian row of palazzos complete with canals and gondoliers on demand if required together with vast rooms filled to the brim with Murano glass, and a palace that looked like a double for the palace of Versailles. There was even park-cum-palace called the Fun Palace with a fantasyland theme and an expansive garden full of perfectly maintained and oiled rides that sat eerily empty, just waiting for someone to push a button.

To Tora they seemed like the folly of a boy who'd never grown up, buildings that lacked the elegant good taste of the Old Palace despite the wealth of treasures they contained, buildings that ventured into the territory of ostentatious display of wealth for wealth's sake.

'Why so many?' she asked Rashid as their convoy left the last on the list, the so-called Fun Palace, a rococo confection based on the retreats of the renaissance royals that wouldn't be out of place in the French countryside. 'Who even needs so many palaces?'

'Malik did,' he said, 'because apparently the harem in the Old Palace was nowhere near big enough.'

'So he built six additional palaces to accommodate his women?'

'Apparently he was a man of insatiable tastes. I can't think how else he could have so happily squandered so much money and so many hours when he should have been working for his people.'

'But he had no children?'

'It didn't stop him from trying,' he said drily, and Tora couldn't help but laugh.

'What?'

'You. You sounded almost funny then.'

'I'm sorry. I didn't mean to.'

'I know,' she said with a grin. 'That's what makes it so funny.'

He looked away, feigning umbrage at her laughter, when in fact he was enjoying himself immensely. It was good to get away from the endless papers and the spreadsheets filled with numbers that showed just how badly the economy had been neglected over the last three decades while its treasury had been plundered to pay for the Emir's follies.

It was good to be with her.

Surprisingly good.

He'd imagined this outing would give her the chance to see him in a better light. He hadn't expected to discover he liked her more in return.

She made a pleasant change from Kareem, who he liked and respected but whose conversation was limited to the necessary and delivered without humour.

Needless to say, she was more appealing on the eyes than Kareem, too. Much more. Today she was wearing another of those silky robes, this one coloured in ripples of yellow and orange so she looked like a shimmering sunset as she walked. He'd been right to ask her along. She made the tour a holiday excursion, expressing delight and sometimes horror at the old Emir's excesses, rather than a dry exercise of checking out the inventory.

And suddenly he didn't want it to end. They were on the outskirts of the city, only a sprinkling of buildings amidst the desert sands, and he had an idea. 'Stop the car,' he told the driver, and the vehicles rolled to a halt. Rashid climbed out to talk to Kareem and a few minutes later he was back and their car peeled away from the others and headed towards the desert proper.

'What's happening?' Tora said. 'Where are we going?'

'Seeing we are so close, I thought we should see something of the desert. Apparently there is an oasis not far from here.'

He saw her bite her lip as she glanced at her watch. 'Will it take long? We've been gone hours already and I feel bad leaving Yousra by herself for too long.' And he felt a pang of admiration for this woman who he could see wasn't using Atiyah as an excuse to get away from him, but was genuinely concerned for his sister.

'It won't take long,' he promised.

It was only a few kilometres further on through the desert sands that they found it, an oasis of palm trees, an island of green amidst the golden landscape, almost empty but for a few families picnicking on and paddling in the shores of a pond alive with waterfowl, its fringes thick with water lilies of white and pink.

'It looks idyllic,' she said as the car pulled into the shade of the palms, and they climbed outside. The desert air was hot and dry, but there was a breeze fanning through the greenery and over the water and Tora's *abaya* fluttered in the warm air as she took in the contrast between desert sands and lush greenery.

'Kareem said this was once a resting place for the caravans that traversed the dunes. Now the city has spread closer and it has been retained as a park for the people of Qajaran.'

'It's beautiful.' She turned to him then, her eyes alive and bright. 'Can we paddle, do you think? Only it's been such a long day and my feet are killing me.'

He wasn't sure why she asked when she was already slipping off her sandals and raising the hem of her *abaya* to slip her feet into the water's edge. 'Oh, it's gorgeous,' she called over her shoulder. 'Bliss. You have to try this for yourself.'

He shook his head, even as he laughed. It was crazy. He swam laps for fitness and he'd been a champion rower along with his desert brothers when he'd been at university, but he wasn't sure he'd ever paddled before. And then, because he figured there was no time like the present, he shucked off his loafers and rolled up the bottom of his trousers and joined her.

She was right. The water was cool and clear and the perfect antidote to hot feet tired from traipsing around half a dozen palaces. Tiny fish darted around his ankles while a crane stood on one leg, watching warily from a distance, and Rashid wondered at the pleasure in such a simple occupation. Tora turned around then and pointed to one of the families whose children were laughing in the shallows at their father holding up a baby whose little feet kicked at the water, giggling gleefully as he splashed himself and everyone around him. 'We should bring Atiyah here for a picnic—what do you think?'

And something shifted enough inside him that it almost sounded like a good idea. He would like to, he thought, if this woman came with them. 'Maybe,' he said as he stepped out of the water and sat on the grassy edge, looking up at the mountains in the distance, and thinking…

She came and sat down next to him. 'Thank you for bringing me here,' she said, flapping at the bottom of her wet hem while she studied the henna designs on her feet as they dried in the warm air. 'That was magic. I don't think you're ever too old to paddle.'

Alongside her he made a sound, half snort, half laughter. 'Just as well, really, given that's my first time.'

Her head swung around. 'Seriously? You've never paddled before?'

'Not that I recall.'

'But when you were a kid—you must have gone to the beach or something?'

He shook his head as he looked out over the water, his elbows on his bent knees. 'The school I went to had a pool. It's not like I didn't learn how to swim.'

But he'd never experienced the simple delights of paddling in the shallows? And she thought back to that night on the terrace when he'd told her he wouldn't send Atiyah off to boarding school, and she wondered. 'How old were you when you were sent to school?'

'I don't remember, I just remember always being there.' He shrugged. 'It was a good school, set in leafy Oxford. I can't complain.'

'But so far from home.'

'That was my home.'

'But your parents?'

'My mother died when I was in infancy. I grew up believing my father was also dead.'

A chill went down Tora's spine. Atiyah was his sister so his father had been alive… It was so horrible, she couldn't help but want it to be untrue. 'You've got to be kidding.'

And he turned and looked at her with eyes that were dark empty holes, and she regretted her words even before he spoke. 'Do you really think I'd kid about a thing like that? No, I never knew he'd been alive all that time until I was summoned to a meeting in Sydney to be told that he'd actually been alive for the thirty years I'd believed him dead, only to have been killed in a car crash weeks before. Not only that though, because I was now the proud guardian of his two-month-old child. How would you feel, learning all that?'

Under the heavy weight of his empty eyes, she knew. Gutted. Devastated. *Angry.*

And her breath caught. He'd been angry the night she'd met him. Because that was the day he'd learned the truth? God, he'd had good reason. No wonder he'd been so resentful of Atiyah, charged with the responsibility of a child of a father who'd as good as abandoned him three decades before.

She looked out over the surface of the water and the ripples that sparkled under a hot sun. 'Why would any man do such a thing to his child?'

Rashid swiped at an insect on his legs. 'Apparently he was protecting me,' he said. 'Protecting both of us.' And he told her of his father being chosen as the Emir's successor, the plot to dispose of both father and child and the exile and separation that had followed.

'And he never once contacted you in all that time.'

'No.'

'So you were brought up by strangers?'

He leaned back on his elbows. 'My houseparents were my guardians. A good couple, I suppose, but I never felt I belonged. I was never part of their family, so much as a responsibility.'

It explained so much about the man he was. No wonder he felt so ill-equipped to care for a child. 'What a hard, cold way to grow up.'

'It wasn't so bad, I guess. What they might have lacked in affection, they made up for in instilling discipline. I was the perfect student in the classroom or on the field.'

Discipline, yes. But no love. No warmth. And her heart went out to the little boy who'd grown up alone and now had the unexpected weight of a country on his shoulders. 'Will you stay, do you think? Will you become the new Emir?'

Rashid sighed. 'I'm not sure,' he said, being honest. 'My father chose not to tell me any of this—I think he valued his freedom in the end, and he wasn't about to force me into a role he saw himself having escaped. Either that, or he thought one attempt on my life was enough.'

'Would it be dangerous?'

'Kareem says not. Apparently the longer Malik ruled, the more of a buffoon he became, interested in satisfying only his own appetites. Everyone knows the last three decades have been wasted. The people want change.'

Rashid stared into the middle distance. Why was he telling her all this? But somehow putting it into words helped. Somehow her questions helped. *Would he stay?*

Qajaran needed help, that much he'd learned these last few days, but was he the man who could turn the country's fortunes around? Zoltan would be here tomorrow to advise him, but there would be no need for that if he decided to walk away.

Could he simply walk away?

And once again his eyes were drawn to the line of mountains that lay across the sands, and he thought about the words Kareem had spoken in an office in Sydney what seemed like a lifetime ago, words that had made no sense to him at the time, words that now played in his mind to the drum beats of his heart.

'Where are you going?' she asked as he rose to his feet and walked towards the sands that lay beyond the fringe of green.

'Just something I need to do,' he said, before stepping from the grass and onto the sands, feeling the crunch of the thin surface give way to the timeless hot grains of Qajaran's sands beneath. Anyone watching would think him mad—Tora must certainly think him mad—but his heart was thumping as he walked, feeling the grains work between his toes and scour his soles. And when he'd walked far enough, he stopped and leaned down to pick up a handful of sand and let it run through his fingers while warm desert air filled his lungs and the breeze tugged at his shirt, whispering the secrets of the ages. He turned his head to listen and found his gaze looking across the desert plains, back to where the blue mountains rose in the distance, and, with a juddering bolt of sensation, he saw the colour of his eyes in the distant range and he felt it then—the heart of Qajaran beating in his soul.

And he knew he was part of this place.

He was home.

His skin still tingling with the enormity of the revelation, he turned back towards the oasis. He was staying. He knew that now, and he wanted to tell Tora, to share it with her because somehow he knew she would understand.

He frowned, because there were more people gathered there where he had left her. They bowed as he drew closer, calling blessings upon him and wishing him well, their eyes full of hope, while Tora stood there in their midst, her beautiful face alight with a smile that warmed his newly found soul.

The children were less hesitant than their parents. They ran up to him, wanting to touch his hand, and he knew he didn't deserve this kind of reception, and he didn't know if he would make a good leader, but the people of Qajaran needed a good leader, and he would try.

The price of failure was too high.

Their return to the Old Palace was subdued, Rashid lost in thought as he watched the desert retreat in the face of the city. Kareem would welcome his decision, he knew, and throw himself into executing the plans for the coronation he already had mapped out. And still he wondered if it was the right decision.

'So what will you do with the palaces?' she asked. 'Unless you're planning on establishing your own harems, of course.'

Lord help him. He couldn't imagine having six women, let alone six harems. One woman was more than enough and he didn't have her. Not really. And there was another problem…

He shook his head, because there were no easy answers to anything. 'I'm not sure. But the state can't keep paying for them. Kareem wanted to show me, in case I preferred one of them over the Old Palace.'

'I like the Old Palace,' she said. 'It has history and character. You have to keep that as the kingdom's base, surely?' And then she paused. 'Not that it has anything to do with me, of course.'

'But that still leaves the problem of what to do with the rest. Qajaran already had a Desert Palace and a Mountain Palace before Malik took it into his head to increase the number of palaces by two hundred per cent.'

'Sell them, then.'

'Not possible. They belong to the people of Qajaran. For better or worse, they are part of their heritage. Even if they could be sold, nobody would pay what Malik spent on them. The country would lose a fortune.'

'So you have six white elephants costing a fortune to upkeep?'

'That's the problem.'

'Could they be turned into boutique hotels? So many bedrooms already with en-suites—surely it couldn't be too hard.'

He looked at her. Really looked at her. 'Did someone tell you that? Did Kareem mention it while we were looking around the palaces?' Kareem had mooted it as a possibility with him just yesterday when he was going over the final details for the inspection.

She shrugged and shook her head. 'No. But what else could you do with them? You could hardly turn them all into museums—that would never pull as many tourists from overseas or earn you as much money. But think of the tourists who would flock here, wanting to tick off staying at Qajaran's quirky hotels one by one, or get married alongside a Venetian canal in the desert. And think of the employment that could be generated in servicing busy hotels rather than in maintaining six empty palaces waiting for their next visit from their Emir.'

He rubbed his chin between his thumb and his fingers, the gravel of his whiskers like a rasp against his skin. The tour had taken the better part of the day and he had a five o'clock shadow to show for it. 'Maybe it's possible.' The palaces couldn't be sold, but they could be leased to a luxury hotel chain to manage…

'Yes!' she said, cutting into his thoughts, 'but not the Fun Palace. That one would be different. You should open that one up to the people of Qajaran. The palace can still be a hotel, but the park should be free for all citizens who just want to visit with their families, not to stay in the rooms.'

'And for those that do,' he said, intrigued, 'they would have to fight the crowds to access the rides that others get free?'

'So give them two hours' exclusive use in the evening or morning. I don't know. It's not exactly my line of expertise. I'm just offering a suggestion. And while you'd probably make money if you converted them all to boutique hotels, it would just be a shame if the Qajarese people couldn't enjoy something that is their own heritage, especially when it's already a fun park.'

Not her line of expertise. So why did what she said make so much sense? Even down to offering the Qajarese people an opportunity to sample the luxury and indulgences they had so unwittingly paid for.

'How did you come to work at Flight Nanny?' he said, wondering about this woman who looked after babies and children and who came up with solutions to problems way outside her apparent field of expertise.

'Simple,' she said. 'Sally and I went through school together and then university. When she and Steve started Flight Nanny, I jumped at the opportunity to join them.'

'They sound like good friends.'

'The best. Sally is like my sister. When my parents died, I was devastated. She kept me going. And then, when I poured my grief into a love affair with Mr Wrong that ended spectacularly badly, she was there to pick up the pieces. I owe her my sanity.'

'What happened,' he asked, 'with this Mr Wrong?'

'It was my fault just as much. I wanted it so much to work out—I needed to love someone enough to compensate for the loss of my parents and I was too needy, too demanding. I can see that now, of course. I can see that when he tried to let me down gently, I wouldn't let him go.'

'So how did it end?'

She gave a wan smile. 'Badly. He announced to the world that he was dumping me on every social media account he was signed up with, because I was "a bitch, a total cow and crap in bed". I do believe those were his exact words. Mind you, they worked.'

'You're not any of those things,' he said, 'for the record.'

She gave a half-smile. 'For the record, I thank you. And I'd rather you didn't post that anywhere, if it's all the same to you.'

It was his turn to smile. The guy was a loser—that much was clear. 'You're better off without him. Anyone who could say those things wasn't worthy of being a friend, let alone a lover, especially when you were already so low.'

'I know. Sally said the same thing.'

'So why child care?' he asked, changing the subject, because the thought of her with another man was suddenly unpalatable and not something he wanted to dwell on.

She shrugged. 'I don't know exactly. But I always loved babies and little kids—maybe because I was an only child and grew up alone. They always fascinated me. When I found out I could make a living working with them, it seemed a no-brainer.'

He nodded, although he wasn't sure he entirely understood. He'd grown up alone and he'd mostly kept to himself. If he hadn't happened upon his three desert brothers, he'd probably still be wandering the world alone.

'Have dinner with me,' he said on a whim, because he realised they were nearing the Old Palace and soon she would excuse herself and take herself off to her apartments and the care of Atiyah and he was suddenly sick of being alone.

She looked flustered, her lips parting and closing as if searching for and not finding any words.

'Just dinner.'

'Um… I have to check on Yousra and Atiyah. We've been gone a long time.'

'So check.'

'And if Yousra has had enough or is tired?'

'Bring Atiyah to dinner with you,' he said, surprising himself that he meant it. 'Bring her anyway,' he added, if that helped. Anything to postpone the time she would close herself off from him again.

She blinked. 'Why are you suddenly being so reasonable?'

He turned to her, careful not to reach out a hand and touch her, as he'd been wanting to all day, to touch the molten sunset of her robe, to feel her heat. In the end, he reached out a hand and wrapped it around hers. No pressure, just a hand hold, warm and true. 'Because I've just had the best day I've had in a long time. And I don't want it to end.'

God, he meant it. Tora's skin bloomed all over. From just the touch of his hand. No, from the import of his words and the dark intent of his eyes. He actually meant it.

And it had been a good day. She'd had a personal tour of six amazing palaces and been both dazzled by their brilliance and appalled at their waste, in the company of a man who knew how to push her buttons, be they physical or emotional, and who now was testing out a new one, one that simply said like.

She was intensely aware they'd just entered the palace gates. Aware they'd soon have doors opened and the outside world would intrude and the moment would be gone—as maybe Rashid himself would be, whisked away to put to rights whatever problem besetting the country next needed addressing.

She didn't want the world to intrude. Not just yet.

There would be time enough for the world later.

'Yes,' she said. 'I will have dinner with you.'

'Good,' he said, drawing her hand to his mouth and pressing his lips to the back of it, while his eyes smiled and warmed her in a place she hadn't expected his eyes to warm. Because it wasn't just sex she saw there, she was sure. There was more.

And she welcomed finding more.

The car slowed, even as her heart raced. Dinner with Rashid. Could they really be friends? After today, she wanted to believe it possible.

He was still holding her hand when the car pulled up to the steps. She liked the feel of her hand in his. She liked the way it made her feel, liked that today their hitherto stumbling relationship had advanced to another level, one that involved both trust and respect.

There was someone there waiting for them, standing on the steps in addition to the guard of honour that seemed to grace their every entry and exit. Someone tall and broad-shouldered with deep black hair and he was looking at their car and smiling.

'Who is that man?' she said, and Rashid looked to where she was indicating.

'Zoltan!' he said, with a wide smile. A man Rashid was clearly beyond excited to see from the way he didn't notice when she slipped her hand from his, and Tora figured the dinner invitation was off.

'Zoltan!' Rashid called as he jumped from the car. 'You're early.'

Rashid ran up the steps and pulled his friend into a hug. 'I was told you were arriving tomorrow.'

Zoltan laughed. 'I thought I'd surprise you.'

'It is a good surprise. Thank you for coming. You don't know what this means to me.'

'To me, too. Whoever thought a humble orphan child turned petroleum and gas billionaire would ever finally make good?' he joked before turning serious. 'You have had a rough ride of it lately, I understand.'

Rashid shook his head. 'I am glad you could come. There is so much to tell you.'

'Tell me over dinner.'

And Rashid suddenly remembered and looked around, to where the cars of the convoy were spilling their contents, but with Tora nowhere to be seen.

'Tora,' he said. He'd asked her to have dinner with him and now she was gone and he felt her absence like a sudden hole in a perfect day.

'What did you say?' Zoltan asked, and Rashid once again felt the jolt of pleasure that his brother was here. It was probably for the best that she'd gone, he thought, given the circumstances. At least it saved an awkward introduction. With any luck, Zoltan wouldn't have heard he was married. He'd save that gem for later. There were more important matters to discuss right now.

'So tell me,' he said, turning his back on the hollow feeling in his gut as he led Zoltan into the palace. 'How are Aisha and the family?'

It was for the best, Tora told herself as she made her way back to her suite. He was so excited to see his friend, he would have regretted asking her to have dinner with him the instant he saw him. Besides, dinner would have been pointless. It was all so pointless. She would be going home soon and leaving this world behind. Why establish links that would have to be broken?

Because when it all came down to it, this wasn't

about her. This was about ensuring a bond between Rashid and Atiyah, and the signs were heartening.

It was enough.

Yousra was waiting for her in her apartments, singing to Atiyah as she rocked the baby's cradle. She looked so relieved when she saw Tora coming, Tora thought the girl was going to burst into tears.

'How was she?' Tora whispered with a frown, peeking over into the cot expecting to find a sleeping child, only to find two dark eyes that immediately locked onto hers and widened before her face crumpled and she started wailing before Tora could duck out of the way.

'I'm so sorry,' she said to Yousra, scooping the child into her arms. 'I shouldn't have left her.' After all the turmoil she'd already suffered, all the losses, Atiyah had grown used to having Tora around, only for Tora to disappear for hours, and her heart was breaking for the little girl. She should never have agreed to go with Rashid.

And she knew she couldn't afford to think that way. Knew that it was wrong. She couldn't afford to become a fixture in this child's life, and yet already it was happening. She should have returned home as she'd been supposed to. She should have handed Atiyah over and walked away. And she would have, if Rashid hadn't come up with this whole crazy marriage deal.

And now the longer she stayed, the harder it would become because the more attached to her Atiyah would become, and one day soon she'd be leaving for good and Atiyah would be hurt all over again.

She swayed as she pressed her lips to Atiyah's soft curls and felt tears sting her own eyes as Atiyah's tears threatened to rip out her heart. Staying longer was such a double-edged sword. It gave Atiyah security for a little while. But it gave Tora more time to fall in love with a precious dark-eyed child.

She'd never felt this way about one of her charges before. She'd never come so close to feeling what a mother must feel—protective and defensive and determined that she should have only the best of everything, including love. But then, she'd never had such a tiny baby to look after.

If only Rashid had been more accepting of his sister in the start. If only she hadn't felt as if she had to compensate, to give Atiyah the love she should have got from him.

Damn.

CHAPTER ELEVEN

NIGHT FELL FAST, the way it seemed to do here, the daylight hurrying away to make way for the night. Atiyah settled the same way, her bellowing cries becoming snuffles and then sniffs and before long sleep had overtaken her. Tora knew she had to wean herself off Atiyah and take a back-seat role in looking after her, but still she sent Yousra to visit her family and have a night off after her trying day. She'd talk to Rashid tomorrow about getting an extra carer then. He was busy with his friend tonight and, besides, for now she was happy to sit back and relax with the meal they'd had sent up to her and check her emails.

She smiled when she found one from Sally with the subject line I love you!

After she'd read the message, she was sniffing and there were tears in her eyes for the second time tonight. Steve was doing all the right things according to his test results and he was ready to be transferred to Germany. Sally had been able to tell the doctors to get the ball rolling.

They wouldn't waste any time now. If all went well and Steve could hang in there, Sally wrote, he'd be on his way within the next day or so towards the treatment that could save his life. And there were no promises, she said, being brave, but it was the only chance he had and they were staying positive and whatever happened, she owed Tora a debt she could never repay.

Happy news, Tora thought, blinking away the tears. The very best kind of news. And she was glad of Rashid's deal now, for all the grief it had caused her, and for all the grief it would inevitably cause her when she had to return home.

It would be worth it if the treatment worked.

It would all be worth it.

'So what's she like, this half-sister of yours?' Zoltan asked, plucking grapes from a bunch on a platter. They were seated on low sofas in one of the palace reception rooms that had doors that opened onto the gardens so that the scent of frangipani wafted in.

'I don't really know,' Rashid said. 'She's a baby.' But then he thought about Tora leading him to Atiyah's cradle to look down upon the sleeping infant and felt a pang of pride. 'She's a cute little thing, though.'

'Huh,' said Zoltan. 'That's all you can say? Spoken like a man who hasn't had children yet. Just wait until you have your own. You won't be so vague about the details then. You'll be hanging out for that first smile and that first tooth.'

Rashid snorted. 'Dream on,' he said, because even if he was warming to the child, he wasn't about to go all gooey over her any time soon. Not like Tora at least, who had been so excited about Atiyah smiling.

'That's where you're wrong, brother,' Zoltan said, waving a grape between his thumb and forefinger for emphasis, 'An Emir needs an heir. So you don't want to wait too long—you're not getting any younger.' He popped the grape between his teeth and crunched down.

Rashid shook his head. Just because he'd had some kind of epiphany out at the oasis today, didn't mean he was looking to ensure there were an heir and a spare any time soon. 'Give me a break, Zoltan. One thing at a time.'

'Not a chance. Now you'll have to find yourself a wife. Last desert brother standing, but not for long. You don't have a choice any more. Your footloose and fancy-free playboy days are toast.'

It was all Rashid could do to stop from blurting the news that in actual fact he *was* married, just to shut his friend up. Because that would be a mistake and there would be no shutting Zoltan up once he learned that particular snippet of information. What was more, he'd be off and running, firing off messages to Bahir and Kadar before they got here, get their wives all excited in the process, and Rashid would never hear the end of it.

No, he had serious stuff to get done before he let that particular cat out of the bag. He didn't want them to know about Tora just yet. He didn't want them making a bigger deal out of it than it was. Let them find out in their own good time—but by then he'd be halfway to sending her home.

Although why that left him suddenly cold, he wasn't entirely sure.

'You make marriage sound such fun,' he said, suddenly grumpy, and not just because he knew for a fact that it wasn't fun and that in his case it was nothing more than the means to an end. 'Anyway,' he said, needing to change the subject, 'I didn't ask you here to talk about my love life. Let's get to work.'

Rashid stood on his terrace, his hands spread wide apart on the balustrade, looking up at the inky sky. Below in the gardens the fountains played and the birds settled in for the night, the world at peace.

While inside him his emotions clashed and raged in a war that had forgotten what peace was. It didn't seem to matter the decision he'd made today, or maybe his emotions clashed because of it.

Duty.

Self-doubt.

Fear.

Duty.

It always came back to duty.

His heart thumped like a drum, a tattoo cursing the ever-present, inescapable duty. His stomach squeezed tight and he inhaled the dark night air in response to the bite of pain. It didn't matter what he'd decided out in the desert today, his first session with Zoltan had given him no comfort. There was so much to do. So much he needed to learn. So many doubts about what was possible to best help this country and its people…

Fear.

He wasn't used to feeling fear.

He had never failed at anything he had put his hand to, but then he had made choices that reflected his desires and wants. He'd decided his path. He'd worked hard and acted on hunches and educated guesses and he'd been successful by taking calculated risks and when those hunches had paid off. But it had always been his choice to do those things and follow that path.

Never before had he been sucked into a bottomless pit from which there was no escaping and where there was no choice.

Duty.

Self-doubt.

Fear.

Together they tangled and churned until his gut felt battered and heaving and one thing emerged victorious from the mayhem, as if that one thing had been lying in wait, ready to step into the void.

Need.

Powerful and insistent, it rose up like a mushroom cloud that reached out to fill every part of him. He turned and looked along the terrace, towards her suite, to where the glow from her lamps spilled into puddles.

Tora.

Talking to her today had been the one thing that had let him make sense of the tangled thoughts in his mind when nothing else had. She had listened and understood. She had shown him the simple fun of paddling.

And he had repaid her by leaving her cold.

And without being aware that he'd made a decision, his feet started walking.

Towards the light.

Towards Tora.

She should be sleeping. She kept telling herself to put the book down, but she was reading a book about Qajaran, about its treasures and its colourful history and the wars and crusades that had touched its shores and crossed its desert borders, and she was fascinated. And being right here, in the Old Palace that had seen so much of what she was reading, brought it all to life.

Just one more chapter, she promised herself as she glanced at the clock and turned the page anyway.

She jumped at the soft rap on the glass, her heart giving a crazy leap in her chest so that she almost didn't hear when the tap came again. She slid from the bed, her feet cool on the marble tiles, and pulled on a robe, because, whoever it was, she wasn't going to be caught on the terrace in just her nightgown again.

'Tora,' she heard, and she didn't know whether to be worried or relieved when she recognised Rashid's voice. 'Are you awake?'

The door to the terrace was open to let in the breeze, but she stayed her side of the filmy curtain, just inside the room, an invisible barrier between them. 'What do you want?'

He shook his head as if he didn't know why he was here, standing outside her door in the middle of the night. 'I don't… No, nothing. I wanted to apologise for how things worked out tonight. For leaving you in the lurch when Zoltan arrived.'

'It's okay. I understand. Your friend would be wanting to catch up with you.'

He nodded. 'And,' he said, his lips pulling to one side as he struggled with the words, his eyes troubled, 'I just wanted to see you.'

Her heart tripped and her breath caught in her throat. Her mind told her it meant nothing—but her heart…her heart wanted to believe the words he had said, just a little. 'I had a good day today, thank you.'

'Good. I didn't have a chance to thank you. For your thoughts. I will speak to Kareem tomorrow.'

And she remembered that she'd wanted to talk to Rashid, too, about changing the arrangements for Atiyah, so that she wouldn't grow too fond of her, but that could wait, because right now the night air wore a velvet glove that stroked her skin, bringing with it the scent of him, warm and musky, masculine and spicy, much like Qajaran itself.

And she remembered another night, and her head on his shoulder, drinking in that scent, thinking it would never get old, that she would never get enough of it.

'What's it like,' he said suddenly into the silence, 'when a baby smiles?'

She blinked at the question, wondering where it had come from when this was a man for whom babies didn't seem to register. 'It's like sunshine in a hug,' she said. 'It's like the world lights up and wraps you in love.'

He nodded, but his eyes looked as conflicted as ever, as if he was warring with himself, and she wondered what he'd made of what she'd said or what he'd expected to hear. 'Good. I would like to see that. I won't keep you any longer.' He turned to leave, but he looked so tortured, this man who had the weight of Qajaran on his shoulders, that she couldn't bear him to go like that, so she touched his forearm.

'Rashid?'

He looked down at her hand as if it were a foreign object. 'Yes?'

She pulled herself up, and pressed her lips to his fevered skin, a kiss that was tender and sweet, a kiss designed to soothe rather than inflame. 'Thank you, for coming by,' she said, before letting go and drawing back into the relative safety of her suite. 'Goodnight.'

He was still too keyed up to sleep. Rashid lingered on the terrace under the soft dark sky lit with its sliver of moon and sprinkle of stars and breathed deeply of the night air, air that came scented with frangipani and the blossom of lemon and lime, the ache in his belly subsided for now, the factions raging inside him finding an uneasy truce.

Only the need remained undiminished.

Need for a woman who gentled away his fears merely by her presence and her own evocative perfume and the press of her lips gentle on his cheek. Need for a woman it had taken every ounce of his self-control not to pull her to him and forcibly satisfy.

The need—and something else he couldn't quite put his finger on.

He went to sleep dreaming of Tora and her honeyed voice that played in his mind over and over, so that he woke with it still in his head.

He asked Kareem when they met over breakfast if he knew it, a lullaby about oranges and apricots and fat pigeons. 'It seems familiar but I cannot work out where I have heard it before.'

Kareem regarded him solemnly, his eyes a little sad. 'You would have heard it, of course. It is a classic Persian lullaby, very popular, very beautiful. It is a song your mother used to sing to you when you were just a baby.'

Sensation skittered down his spine like spiders' legs. 'But my mother died when I was just a few months old. Surely I couldn't remember that?'

The older man shrugged. 'Perhaps your father sang it after she was gone. Who can say? But it is something left to you from your parents—a link to your past—something to be treasured.'

He sat back in his chair with his hand to his head. Treasured? For the life of him he couldn't picture himself with his father, let alone imagine his father singing him a lullaby. He might have believed it once, but not now. It didn't fit with a man who had hidden himself from his son for thirty years.

Kareem smiled sadly. 'He loved you, Rashid. I know that it is hard for you to believe, but, for better or for worse, he did what he had to do. As you, his son, have to do.'

Rashid sighed.

His father loved him? Why did he have such a hard time believing it?

'So when can I meet her?' Zoltan asked after a heavy morning going through protocols and affairs of state with Rashid and Kareem and the Council of Elders.

Rashid's first thought was of Tora. Her kiss had haunted him last night, as he had lain on his bed waiting for sleep to claim him, her kiss and the feel of her smooth fingers on his arm and her wide cognac eyes.

'Why do you want to meet her?'

'Well, she is your sister, isn't she? You don't have to keep her locked away in a cupboard somewhere. You do let her see the light of day sometimes, don't you?'

'Oh, Atiyah,' he said, struck by Zoltan's words, because once again Tora had said something similar.

'Who did you think I meant?' asked Zoltan, and his friend looked at him as if he thought he was losing it in the desert heat.

Maybe he was. He blinked. 'I'll send for her,' he said easily, because it was a good idea, because it meant he would see Tora again, and after last night's sweet encounter he yearned to.

But when Atiyah arrived, it was not Tora's arms that bore her but Yousra's instead, and he felt a piercing stab of disappointment.

'Oh, Rashid,' Zoltan said, 'what a beauty,' and he surprised the other man by taking the baby and holding her in front of him to look at her properly. Atiyah's dark eyes were wide and uncertain, the bottom lip of her little Cupid's-bow mouth ready to start quivering. But before it could, he had the child tucked into his arms and was sitting down on the sofa again, and Rashid blinked at the ease with which he handled the child. To him she was too small, too full of traps for the unwary. 'You are going to have your work cut out for you when she becomes a young woman.'

Was he? Something else to look forward to. Wonderful.

The baby started fussing and squirming but Zoltan remained unfazed and uncovered her tiny toes and stroked the bottom of her feet with his middle finger. Tiny feet, thought Rashid, looking on, struck by life in miniature.

'Are you ticklish, little one?' Zoltan said, and Atiyah's little legs started pumping, chuckles now interspersed with her complaints. For a while it looked as if Zoltan had the baby's measure, but soon her face became redder and more screwed up and the chuckles gave way to her cries.

'Whoa,' said Zoltan, admitting defeat as her cries became bellows. 'I think it's time you went to your big brother, little one.'

And before he could say no, his tiny sister had been deposited into his hands. He stared down at the squawking bundle in his lap, wondering at the weight and her energy and the power of her lungs.

His sister.

His blood.

Who looked nothing like she had when she'd been sleeping.

And his gut churned anew as he tried unsuccessfully to quieten her.

There was no quietening her. The baby screamed and no wonder. Because what did he have to offer her? He knew nothing of what a baby would need. He had no experience—nothing but the shred of a lullaby...

'Yousra!' he snapped to the young woman who was watching helplessly on. 'Take Atiyah. There is somewhere I have to be.'

Zoltan frowned as Yousra took the child.

'Don't we have the next meeting with the council coming up shortly?'

'I won't be long.'

Tora's blood spiked with heat when she saw the name pop into her inbox. She had half a mind to delete the message straight away but the subject header stalled her—Good news.

What would he think would be good news to her—unless he'd had a change of fortunes or mind and somehow managed to recover her funds? She opened the message.

Dear Cousin Vicky

An opportunity's just come up to make some quick money, so obviously I thought of you!

I'm expecting some funds to come in and meanwhile they're promised elsewhere. I need half a million dollars fast, just to tide me over, and wondered if you might mortgage your flat for a couple of weeks to help me out? It's only temporary until those funds come in, and the good news is I'll be able to pay you a one-hundred-thousand-dollar fee guaranteed.

Let me know ASAP.

Your cousin

Matt

PS Like your folks used to say, blood is thicker than water after all!

Good news? Tora stared incredulously at the screen. Her cousin must think her stupid. First he screwed her out of her inheritance and then he wanted her home? Pigs might fly. And as for blood being thicker than water—after the way he'd betrayed the trust of her parents and of her, he was no family to her at all.

She was about to hit the delete button and send the message to the trash where it belonged. 'ASAP' be damned—let him wait for an answer that would never come.

And then she had a better idea. Much better.

So she hit Reply and changed the subject header to Better News! and started typing.

Dear Matt...

She added kisses at the end and then deleted them. No point laying it on too thick. She'd just hit Send with a satisfying click when another message pinged into her inbox. This time she was eager to open it.

We're on our way! Sally wrote. Next stop, Germany!

Yes! She fired off a quick 'good luck' reply and this time added plenty of kisses before she sent it off with a sigh. At least that was going right.

'Tora,' she heard Rashid bellowing from somewhere inside her suite. 'Tora!' He appeared at the doorway to the terrace. 'What are you doing out here?'

'You couldn't just knock like a normal person?' she said drily, wondering where the fire was.

'Why didn't you bring Atiyah when I asked for her?'

'Because you summoned Atiyah, not me. And Yousra is perfectly capable of delivering a child for your inspection. She did bring you Atiyah?'

'Yes, but that's not the point. You should have brought her.'

'Why?'

'Because you're her nanny. She's your responsibility.'

'No, Rashid. She's *your* responsibility, but you like to pass it off to me and that's a bad thing.'

'Why?'

'Because she's becoming dependent on me. She's bonding. Yesterday when I came home from our day out, Yousra was exhausted from trying to settle her.'

'She started screaming when Yousra brought her down.'

They heard her coming, still crying as Yousra entered the apartments. 'I'm sorry, Sheikha,' the young woman said as Tora went to meet her, taking the child and hugging her to her chest.

'It's okay,' Tora said, to both the baby and

Yousra as Atiyah grabbed her hair in her tiny hands and her tears soaked her gown. 'It's okay.' Tora sent Yousra off to fetch some warm milk as the baby snuffled into her, her cries slowly abating.

'You see,' she said, speaking softly to Rashid as she swayed. 'I had to send her with Yousra as she's become too attached to me. You need to get more carers or take care of her yourself.'

He looked taken aback. 'But if she feels safe with you—'

'I'm leaving, Rashid. Going home as soon as our marriage can be dissolved. Or had you forgotten?'

He shook his head. 'So stay longer if Atiyah needs you. Do you need to go back straight away?'

'Stay for how long? And then what? She grows even more dependent on me. How is that going to work? That's no kind of solution.'

'How much would it take to make you change your mind?'

She sighed as Yousra returned with the milk. 'You know, Rashid, there are some things in the world that money can't fix.'

'Then show me how to do that,' he growled as Tora sat down to feed Atiyah. 'Show me how to hold her so she doesn't cry.'

Tora blinked up at him. 'Do you really mean it?'

'Of course, I mean it. She is my sister. How do you think it makes me look if I do not know how to hold her?'

And Tora looked down at the infant, still snuffling, her eyes red-rimmed and puffy from crying. She could say no now, to save Atiyah any more distress, but that would be fair to neither of them. So instead she waited until the baby was a little more relaxed, her eyelids fluttering closed as she drank. 'Then sit down and I'll pass her over to you and maybe she won't notice.'

Neither of them really believed that, but Rashid did as she suggested and Tora gently passed the baby over. Atiyah instantly jolted into awareness, her eyes wide open, her feeding stopped as she worked out what had changed in her world. 'It's okay, Atiyah, you're safe,' Tora crooned, even as she tried to show him how better to cradle the infant by relaxing and softening his arms.

Atiyah wasn't convinced and in the end they both conceded defeat, letting Tora take her back.

'I can't stay,' he said. 'I have to go.'

Tora nodded, rocking the child in her arms a little as Atiyah resumed feeding, keeping her eyes open this time for any more tricks. 'I know,' she said. 'It will get easier, I promise,' and she couldn't help smiling as he left, because Rashid had tried.

* * *

Tora's words stayed with him as he made his way back through the palace to the meeting on foreign policy with a heavy heart made heavier by the fact that nothing seemed to work with Atiyah, even when he wanted it to. He'd tried. By God, he'd tried to do all the things Tora had told him, to relax and yet hold her securely so that she'd felt safe, to sway her gently without jerking, to comfort her.

'There are some things in the world that money can't fix.' Didn't he know it? She was preaching to the converted there. There was no amount of money he could throw at the predicament he was in and make it go away.

But surely her case was different. Why did she have to go? If she really cared about Atiyah and didn't want to upset her, surely she could agree to stay a bit longer. She didn't have to rush off. At least to give him enough time to get used to his new responsibilities.

Besides, he was intrigued by her, this woman who could be temptress, Madonna, businesswoman and even comforter. As she'd comforted him last night when he'd gone to her room with her quiet words and her sympathetic eyes.

And he didn't want her to go.

Not yet.

'Ah,' said Kareem coming out of the meeting

room he was just heading into. 'We have been waiting for you to begin.'

And Rashid knew what she'd said was right. No amount of money in the world could help him now.

Tora and Yousra were sitting in the Pavilion of Mahabbah the next morning where it was still deliciously cool alongside the lake, a soft breeze stirring the curtains. Atiyah lay on a rug on her stomach on the floor attempting mini push-ups on her chubby arms. Tora was keeping out of her line of sight, but every now and then the baby would look around until she found her before resuming her exercises, assuring herself that, yes, Tora was still there. She was so alert and way too knowing for such a small bundle, Tora thought, and she was just about to disappear for a walk around the garden to see if she might forget, even for a little while, when they heard the voices, young and older.

Through the gossamer curtains Tora could see the three women, two striking dark-haired beauties and one blonde and equally stunning, heading towards the pavilion with a clutch of children in tow.

'It looks like we have visitors,' she said to Yousra. 'Do you know who they are?'

'No,' the other woman said, watching their progress. 'I've never seen them before.'

Tora forgot about hiding and scooped up Atiyah from the floor, the child gumming at her fist as the women hovered at the door. 'We're sorry to intrude, but we were told we'd find Atiyah here. We couldn't wait to meet her.'

'This is Atiyah,' said Tora, holding the baby in her lap.

'Oh, she's gorgeous,' said the first, coming closer. 'You must excuse us. We've been so excited since we heard the news that Rashid had a baby sister. We're the wives of Rashid's desert brothers—his good friends—and we've arrived for the coronation. I'm Aisha, wife to Zoltan, who has been here advising Rashid, and this is my sister Marina, wife to Bahir, and Amber, wife to Kadar. And these,' she said, gesturing to the active group around her, 'are our children.'

'It's lovely to meet you,' said Tora, introducing herself, feeling a little overwhelmed but delighted too that Atiyah would have more distractions over the coming days. There were three toddlers and two children a little older, a girl and a boy. Other children would be the best entertainment of all. Already she was watching them eagerly, smiling when they came to say hello to her, kicking her little legs with delight.

'One more baby for the desert brothers tribe,' laughed the second dark-haired woman called Marina who was kneeling down and holding

Atiyah's hands. 'And now the children have an aunty. Hello, little Atiyah,' she said with a broad smile, earning one back from the infant.

'You're Australian,' said the blonde woman called Amber, who settled herself down on the sofa next to Tora, a sizeable bump under her dress. 'Me, too. Where are you from?'

'Sydney,' Tora said.

'I'm from Melbourne.'

'And now you live—somewhere around here?'

'Kadar and I live mostly in Istanbul. We were married six months ago.' She smiled. 'It's kind of a long story.' She patted her stomach and her smile widened. 'We're expecting our own first baby in a few months. But how did you end up here, looking after Atiyah?'

It was Tora's turn to smile. 'That's kind of a long story, too. But I'm only here temporarily. I'll be going home soon.'

'Oh,' said Aisha, exchanging glances with the other women, 'for a moment I thought—I was hoping…'

'We were all hoping,' her sister said. 'As soon as we saw you, we were hoping. Rashid needs a good woman, and we thought, maybe he has found one at last.'

'He's the only desert brother left,' added Amber, 'and now he will need a woman by his side, more than ever.'

Tora said nothing, just bounced Atiyah on her knee, silently cursing this stupid marriage and the position it put her in, because it wasn't her place to say anything. Just then the peacocks put in an appearance and distracted everyone and the conversation changed direction and Tora could breathe again and enjoy being in the company of other women.

They drank honey tea and laughed and talked of their children and their husbands. They were bright and beautiful like butterflies in the garden and Tora found herself wishing she could be one of them, but that would mean marrying Rashid for real.

'Forgive me for interrupting,' Kareem said, appearing at the doorway to the pavilion with a gracious bow, 'but His Excellency would like to see you privately, Sheikha Victoria.'

Aisha's ears pricked up first. 'Sheikha?'

'I thought that's what he said,' Marina said.

Amber was staring at her strangely. 'But wouldn't that mean…?'

Tora shook her head, excusing herself as she swept past them, her face ablaze with heat. 'It's not what you think…'

'I've been thinking,' said Rashid a few minutes later, rubbing his chin as he paced the Persian rug in his big study, 'now that my friends are here with their wives and families, we need to be careful about them getting the wrong idea about us.'

He paced the other way. 'I know my friends and they'll blow it out of all proportion so I've decided it's best if I ask Kareem to be careful how he addresses you and I tell them that you're simply filling in for the role of my consort for the coronation. I think it's better that they don't know about the marriage at all.'

He suddenly stopped pacing and looked up at her, his eyes panicked. 'What do you think?'

Tora swallowed as she stood there, her fingers tangling as she selected her words carefully. 'I think it might actually be a bit late for that.'

CHAPTER TWELVE

'WHAT?' ZOLTAN'S HEAD swivelled from Aisha to Rashid when the women joined them before lunch. 'You're already married? You sly dog! And you made out like it was the furthest thing from your mind.'

'But it is!'

'So how does that work when you're already married?'

'Because it's not a real marriage!'

'I want to know how come you didn't invite your best friends?' demanded Bahir.

'Yeah,' Kadar said. 'We invited you to our weddings.'

'Right, you really want to know why I didn't invite you to my fake marriage? Maybe it's because Kareem married us in the plane on the way over here. Sorry, but when you're flying at forty thousand feet it makes it a bit awkward to get the wedding invitations out.'

'But when we were talking before, you acted as if you weren't married at all,' said Zoltan. 'Like anything like that happening was years away.'

'Did any of you guys hear me? It's not a real

marriage!' He gave a long sigh. He'd known this would happen. He'd damn well known it. 'Look, I had to marry someone, in order to adopt Atiyah.'

'Why did you have to adopt Atiyah?' asked Marina. 'She's your sister, isn't she?'

'Yes, but our father was supposed to have died in a helicopter crash thirty years ago and the people believe that and— Oh, what the hell does it matter why? Kareem said she had to be adopted and in order to do that, I had to be married. End of story.'

'Hardly!' snorted Bahir. 'We're just getting to the good stuff. So this woman volunteered to marry you to get you out of a tight spot, did she?'

'Tora,' said Aisha. 'Her name is Tora. I like her.'

'Me, too,' said her sister. 'And she's gorgeous.'

'She's Australian,' chimed in Amber with a grin. 'What's not to love?'

'Agreed,' said Kadar, giving his wife a squeeze as he kissed her cheek. 'This Tora must be some kind of a masochist to volunteer to marry you. What was in it for her?'

'What do you mean, what was in it for her?'

'What, she did it out of the goodness of her heart?'

'I bet it wasn't for his bedside manner.'

'Maybe it was,' suggested Kadar.

'Okay, okay,' said Rashid, who'd had enough, holding up one hand to silence his friends. 'So there may have been a financial inducement involved. We made a deal. So what?'

'Alas, poor Rashid,' Zoltan said with his hand over his heart. 'Unloved and unwanted, left on the shelf, the only one of the desert brothers who actually had to resort to paying a woman to get her to marry him.'

'Give me a break,' growled Rashid. 'Don't you guys make out you wrote the guidebook on romance—we all know that's a lie.'

'But none of us had to break out the chequebook.'

Aisha looked around. 'Why isn't Tora here? You did invite her to have lunch with us, didn't you?'

He rolled his eyes.

'You didn't!' said Marina, eyes wide with accusation. 'Don't tell me you treat her like the hired help?'

'She *is* the hired help.' But that wasn't true either, he had to concede. She was more than that. Much more. He just didn't know what to do about it. 'Anyway, I did invite her to lunch and she declined—said she didn't want to get in the way of a desert-brothers-and-their-families reunion. Is that good enough for you?'

Nobody else thought so, which was why one minute later he was on his way to insist Tora join them for lunch.

* * *

Tora turned off her tablet still smiling. Sally had emailed with the news that Steve was installed at the clinic and that treatment had commenced and to keep her fingers and toes crossed.

Good news. She sent up a silent prayer. At least something was going right at last.

'Excuse me, Tora,' Yousra said. 'His Excellency is here to see you.'

Tora braced herself. She'd known there'd be a fallout from his friends discovering about the marriage, although for the life of her she couldn't believe how he had ever thought he'd manage to keep them from finding out.

She expected anger. What she didn't expect was him insisting she join him and his desert brothers and their wives for lunch.

'Are you sure?' she said. 'It won't give them the wrong idea?'

'They've already got the wrong idea. How about we prove them wrong and show them there's nothing going on? Besides,' he added, 'it seems you're a hit with the women. They threatened that if I failed to bring you back, then they would come and bodily drag you to lunch themselves.'

She laughed. 'In that case, how can I refuse?'

'Did you want to bring Atiyah?'

Tora shook her head. 'Yousra will have no

problem. Atiyah had so much fun with the children this morning, she'll probably sleep for a week. I think the children coming is the best thing that could have happened.'

'Speaking of Atiyah,' he said as they walked down the passageway, past fabulous treasures, brightly coloured urns and dishes set in recesses in the walls, 'have you thought any more about staying on? At least until you can give me some more lessons in handling her.'

Tora sucked in a lungful of air. She hadn't for a moment believed he'd been serious when he'd suggested it and no, she hadn't given it any more thought. She couldn't stay longer and he couldn't expect her to. It wasn't fair on Atiyah and it certainly wasn't fair on her.

As it was, she was struggling to remember all the reasons she shouldn't care about Rashid. She was only a temporary fixture but the longer she was here, the more she liked him. And she didn't want to feel that way, not when it would make it harder to forget him when she was gone.

Not when it would be easier to resist him…

'Rashid—'

'No,' he said, stopping her just shy of the doors beyond which his friends waited, 'don't say anything now. Take your time to think about it. I do want the best for Atiyah, even if it doesn't seem like it. I'm learning, Tora, what she needs. Maybe too slowly for your liking, but I am determined to do right by her.'

He took her hand then, wrapping it between his own, warming her skin as his eyes were warm and tugging on her heart.

'Just promise me you'll think about it. I know it's asking a lot but I won't expect you to stay for nothing. We can work something out.

'What I want now is for Atiyah to feel secure, and she feels secure with you. So will you think about it? Will you think about what it would take to make you stay—even just a little longer?'

Tora looked up at this man, who once she thought was hard and unflinching, arrogant and overbearing, but who she knew to be trying his best.

'I'll think about it,' she promised, although she knew that whatever it would take to make her stay was nothing to how much it would ultimately cost.

'Finally,' came the cry from inside when Rashid opened the door. 'We were about to send out a posse.'

'Welcome, Tora, come and join us,' said another. 'At last, some adult company for you. It will make a nice change from Rashid, I am sure.'

Tora smiled and looked at Rashid, who was scowling. 'My desert brothers,' he said, introducing the three men, 'whom I love with my life. Apart from the times I want to kill them, that is.'

* * *

Coronation day dawned pink and clear and just about perfect, he supposed, if you didn't have a spiked cannonball rolling around in your gut.

Rashid rose early, knowing there was no putting it off, watching the layers of the early-morning sky peel away from where he took coffee on his terrace, pink giving way to blue, just as peace would give way to madness.

The day would be long—interminable at times, no doubt—a breakfast with foreign dignitaries and officials and then a long tortuous motorcade through the city to show off their new Emir before a public feast in Qajaran City's biggest square. Then while the official party headed to the formal coronation ceremony, the gates of the Fun Palace would be thrown open to the public, the ceremony relayed on big screens, before a state dinner for six hundred, all topped off with cannon fire and fireworks.

He was exhausted already.

Exhausted and still more than a little daunted.

His cup rattled against his saucer when he went to pick it up and he lifted his trembling hand to inspect it.

God, what was wrong with him? He had studied the books. He had read the histories and pored over enough economic papers and reports to sink a ship, he had listened to the advice of Kareem and Zoltan and the Council of Elders, and still he wondered what he was doing here.

Duty.

There came a knock at the door and Kareem entered with two assistants bearing the robes he would wear today. 'Excellency, it is time to prepare.'

He was dressed and taking his last few breaths as a free man when he heard the soft knock, but it wasn't Kareem this time. It came from the connecting door to Tora's apartments, the door he had never opened although temptation in the shape of a seductress lay just the other side. The door opened and a soft voice called his name, a voice that, to his fevered mind, sounded as cool as a waterfall. And then she entered, and for a moment he forgot the pain and the fever and the damnable tremble in his hands, because he had never seen anyone more beautiful.

She was dressed in a golden robe, exquisitely embroidered, with gold trim similar to his own, and with long sweeping cuffs on the sleeves and a gossamer-thin silk shawl over her hair that framed her face and floated like a cloud as she moved. She looked like something out of a medieval fantasy.

His next fantasy.

'Rashid,' she said, and her eyes opened wide

as they took in the sight of him dressed in his unfamiliar robes, the first time she had seen him dressed this way. She blinked and seemed to gather herself. 'I just wanted to wish you well today,' she said, 'before it all gets crazy.'

As they both knew it would.

He nodded, because his jaw set too tight to talk and the spiked cannonball in his gut rolled and stuck its spikes in his innards, and he had to take himself to the window to ease the pressure.

For her gesture, her simple act of kindness, had almost brought him undone.

She understood a lot for a woman who wouldn't be here if he hadn't needed to adopt Atiyah and coerced her into a convenient marriage. Because she had become so much more than simply a convenient wife. Her suggestion of opening the Fun Palace to the public had led to its inclusion in the proceedings today, an inclusion he had been informed had been met by the people with huge anticipation and great excitement. He was sharing some of the riches of the state and it was he who was being lauded for it.

She understood a lot more than he had given her credit for.

She would be gone soon.

And his breath caught, as the pointed barbs of that cannonball stuck their points into his raw and wounded flesh anew.

* * *

Tora had never seen Rashid in robes—had never imagined that a man who was so at home and looked so good in western clothes could own a look so traditional and yet he did. His snowy white robes and the tunic beneath were lined with gold trim, his headpiece bound with a band of black that would be replaced with a band of gold, in the final step of the ceremony that would make him Emir.

Tall and broad-shouldered, his skin looking as if it had been burnished by the sun against so much white, he looked magnificent, as if he had been born of the desert sands—born to rule—and yet Tora could see the battle going on behind his features, could see the slight tremble in his hands that he was at pains to disguise, and she ached for him.

'You have no need to be afraid,' she said softly.

'What?' He turned sharply.

'You have no reason to fear.'

'Is that what you think? That I'm afraid?' But his voice lacked the conviction of his words and he knew it by the way he dropped his head and turned away again.

'You're strong,' she said behind him. 'You're intelligent and just and a good man, and you want to do the best for the people of Qajaran. They are lucky to have you.'

He heaved in air, and his words, when they came, might have been blasted raw by the desert sands and the hot wind. 'I was not brought up for this.'

'But it's in your blood. Your father—'

'How is finding you're suddenly responsible for the welfare and futures of millions of people in your blood?'

'You can do this, Rashid,' she said, more sternly than she'd planned. 'You would not be here if you did not believe that. Nobody who knows you, nobody here in this palace does not believe that.'

'How can you—someone who I have known for the tiniest fraction of my life—say that?'

'Because I have seen how hard you work. I have seen that a weaker man would walk away and that a greedy man would stay even if the task was beyond him. You are not like that. You can do this, and you will prevail and you will be a good Emir.'

Kareem interrupted them with a knock on the door. 'Excellency, Sheikha, if you are ready?'

She glanced at him one more time before nodding and saying she would check on Yousra and Atiyah, and had turned to go when he caught her hand before she could disappear. 'Thank you for those words. They mean more than you know.' He squeezed her hand tightly in his before he let her go. 'I just hope you are right.'

She smiled up at him in a way that warmed him from the inside out in a way the sun had never done. 'I know I am,' she said, and her words and her warmth gave him the courage to believe it.

It was exhausting but it was exciting, too. Tora sat alongside Rashid on a sofa under the shade of a tent that had been set up on a dais before a huge square that was full of the longest tables she had ever seen. They had breakfasted with the foreign dignitaries at the palace and now it was the turn of the people to meet their soon-to-be Emir before they returned to the palace for the coronation proper. Bright banners in the Qajarese colours fluttered in the air, competing with the cheerful holiday colours worn by the women and even some of the men. There was a party atmosphere as the feasting got under way, musicians and dancers providing the entertainment, and the sound of laughter was everywhere.

And not even the knowledge that theirs was a marriage of convenience, and that soon she would be heading home and no longer the sheikha, could not diminish her delight in being part of the proceedings. For now, legally at least, she was the sheikha and she would do the best job she could, even if her stomach was a mass of butterflies. But this wasn't about her, it was about Rashid, and the coronation of a new Emir, and it was a once-in-a-lifetime experience and she was going to lap up every single moment of it.

And then a young girl climbed from her seat and approached the dais, in her hands a posy of flowers, her eyes wide and a little in awe as she stood waiting at the steps. Kareem leaned low over Tora's shoulder. 'She has flowers to welcome the new sheikha, if you so wish.'

'For me?' Today was supposed to be all about Rashid, she had thought. But still she smiled and held out her hand to urge her up and the little girl smiled back and climbed the stairs and bowed before handing over the flowers and uttering something in Qajarese.

'What did she say?'

Kareem leaned low again. 'She wished you many sons and daughters.'

'Oh,' Tora said, suddenly embarrassed, before adding *thank you* in Qajarese, one of the few words that she'd learned, feeling guilty because now she wasn't just observing the proceedings; she was a participant in them.

There were more children after that, and more blessings and more flowers, until their table was transformed into a sea of flowers, and Tora smiled at all comers, girl or boy, and their faces lit up when she thanked them.

She glanced across at Rashid at one stage and felt a sizzle down her spine when she found him watching her, his gaze thoughtful and filled with something that almost looked like respect.

Rashid watched her accept another bunch of flowers, touching her fingers to the child's face as she thanked her, and the girl skipped back to where her family were sitting, almost luminescent with delight. Tora was a stranger to this pomp and ceremony as much as he was, an observer caught up in a world not her own, but you wouldn't know it.

She was a natural with the children just as she was a constant for him, always at his side, looking calm and serene and so beautiful that his heart ached. And it was hot and there were hours to go before they could escape, and she so easily could have resented having to take part in the ceremony at all when she was no real wife of his, but she made it look easy.

She made him think anything was possible.

He could do much worse for a wife.

And later, when they were back at the palace during the coronation, when Kareem removed his black headband and lifted the gold *igal* to replace it, it was her words from this morning that he remembered. *'You're strong... You will be a good Emir.'*

Kareem then uttered the ancient words to install him and placed the crown on his head and it was done. He was the Emir.

Cheers and applause broke out across the banquet room, the loudest coming from the quarter where his desert brothers and their families were sitting, and he smiled as he let go a breath he hadn't realised he'd been holding.

He turned to her and saw the moisture there in her eyes—*the tears she'd shed for him*—and he was moved beyond measure.

But before he could tell her, before he could thank her for this morning's words and for her quiet strength today, first there was another feast, another party complete with cannon fire and fireworks, a display above the palace that was echoed all over the city and in the tiny desert and mountain villages of Qajaran.

It was after midnight by the time the festivities wound down. Yousra had taken Atiyah back to her bed hours ago—a day of formalities interspersed with playing with the children had worn her out—and now Rashid walked silently beside Tora towards their suites.

And it seemed to Tora that the very air around them was shimmering, there had been so much energy generated by the celebrations of today, energy that now turned the air electric as they moved, into currents charged by every swish of robe against robe, every slap of leather against the marble floor a metronome, beating out the time she had left.

And all she knew was she didn't want this night to end. She didn't want this feeling to end—this feeling of being at peace with Rashid, of being part of his life…an important part…if only for a day. She wanted to preserve the magic of this moment and hold it precious to her for ever.

For soon her time in Qajaran would be over. Soon she would be back in Sydney in her black skirt and buttoned-up shirt and there would be no more robes of silk to slide against her skin, no more frangipani on the air.

No more Rashid.

Her heart grew tight in her chest.

He was nothing to her really. A roll in the hay and then a quick buck—a deal made with the devil—with plenty of grief along the way. He was nothing to her—and yet her heart had swelled in her chest when he was crowned, she'd been so very proud.

Nothing to her?

And her heart tripped over itself in its rush to tell her she was a liar.

All too soon, it seemed, they were at the door that led to her apartments and she turned and looked up at him, so handsome in his robes, his features a play of dark and shadow against the stark white, the gold *igal* on his head gleaming in the low light. ‘Thank you for seeing me to my rooms.’

He shook his head. ‘It is you who deserves thanking, Tora. What you said to me this morning…’ He trailed off, searching for the words, and she put a finger to his lips.

‘I didn’t say anything you didn’t already know. Maybe you just needed to hear them.’

He caught her hand and pressed it hard against his mouth. ‘You are a remarkable woman, Tora.’

‘No, Rashid.’

‘Yes, you know it’s true. From the moment you arrived, you have impressed everyone you have met.

‘Today, you were the star of the show, charming everyone from the tiniest child to the most important dignitary. I know our hasty marriage was foisted upon you and unwanted, but you have been one of the highlights of my return to Qajaran.’

‘We had a deal, Rashid, remember? I got something out of it, too. The money—it helped a friend of mine out at a tough time.’

‘It was nothing compared to all you’ve done. I owe you, Tora. I don’t know how I can possibly repay you.’

And she knew that the moment was now, that if she wanted this night to continue she would have to be the one to make it so.

She looked up at him, at his dark eyes and his beautiful tortured features, and knew that when she left she would be leaving a part of herself right here in Qajaran.

Her heart.

'Make love with me, Rashid.'

CHAPTER THIRTEEN

THE GROWL RUMBLED up from low in his throat. But then words wouldn't come close to how he was feeling right now. He swept her into his arms and pressed his lips to hers before he carried her through to his suite where he scattered coloured cushions in all directions with one hand before he laid her reverentially in the centre of his bed.

There was no rushing as there had been that first night together. No stripping of clothes separately before they came together. This time Rashid undressed her as if he were opening a gift, taking his time to expose each part of her skin, worshipping it with his lips and his mouth—the hennaed patterns of her hands and feet, the insides of her elbows and the backs of her knees—until she was quivering with desire and need before he'd even slipped her golden *abaya* over her head.

Breath hissed through his teeth when he looked down on her. 'You're beautiful,' he told her with his words and with his adoring eyes, and warmth bloomed inside her. She felt beautiful when he looked at her that way.

He shed his robes and turned from desert ruler into her ruler. Tonight she was his kingdom and his most loyal subject. Tonight she was his queen. Tonight she was his, utterly and completely, and he gave her everything in return.

They made slow, sweet love, long into the night. Making love, she thought, not sex this time, for that tiny seed of a connection had grown into something more, something richer and more powerful.

Love.

And the thought simultaneously terrified and thrilled her, but tonight it seemed so right. She loved him.

And when he followed her into ecstasy and she heard him cry out her name on his lips, she knew he must love her, too, even just a little.

He pulled her close and kissed her and it didn't matter that he was sleeping like the dead less than a minute later. In just one night, he'd given her more than she could have ever wished for.

'I love you,' she whispered, testing the words, touching his lips with hers, before she snuggled closer and closed her eyes, still smiling.

There was a noise from beyond the interconnecting door. A cry. *Atiyah.* Tora listened in the dark, waiting, and a few seconds later came another cry, more insistent this time. Tora strained to hear Yousra's footfall on the tiled floor but heard nothing and Atiyah was working herself up to full throttle now.

Beside her Rashid slept on. He would be exhausted after the strain of the coronation and the physical excesses that followed. She should leave it to Yousra but she didn't want Rashid to be woken, so she rose from the bed, pulling on Rashid's oversized robe, and slipping into her suite.

She scooped Atiyah from her cot and held her to her chest. 'What's wrong, little one? What's the matter?'

Yousra appeared looking ill with dark shadows under her eyes and Tora sent her straight back to bed. Rashid would have to find another carer to share the load now.

Tora checked the baby's nappy and made sure there was nothing pressing in her clothes or bedding. A nightmare, she guessed, just something that spooked her in her sleep. The baby whimpered and snuffled against her chest and she massaged her back and started singing the lullaby she liked to sing to Atiyah. Eventually the little fingers of the fist holding on so tightly to her robe finally relaxed as she drifted back to sleep.

'Where did you learn that song?'

She started and turned, the baby still in her

arms, to find him standing there, a towel lashed low on his hips. 'You're awake.'

'That song,' he said. 'It's beautiful. How do you know it?'

'I learnt it at the child-care centre where I worked. We had children whose families came from all over the world and we tried to learn songs from most of the major languages, even though we were never quite sure of the words.'

'Did you know it was Persian?'

She looked up at him. 'I knew it was Middle Eeastern. Why do you ask?'

'Because I've heard it before. Apparently my mother used to sing it to me. And maybe my father, too. I'd forgotten it until I heard you singing it to Atiyah, that first night on the plane.'

She stilled at his side, her heart going out to him. She couldn't begin to imagine how it must feel—the pain on discovering your parent had been alive all those years you'd thought him dead. The betrayal and the hurt would be almost too much to bear.

'Your father must have loved you a lot,' she said.

He sniffed. 'How do you figure that?'

'Because he left you Atiyah,' she said, trying to find some way of soothing his pain. 'I read that her name means gift. He left you questions without answers, I know, but he left you Atiyah, and the gift of joy and love as well, if you will only see it. He must have loved you to have entrusted her in your care.'

He blinked and reached out a hand to touch Atiyah's curls.

She watched his hand, saw the moment man connected with sleeping child, saw wonder on his face in the low lamp light, and felt a rush of joy. Baby steps, she thought, it would take one baby step at a time. But in time, she knew, he would learn to love Atiyah as he should.

She kissed the baby on the head and tucked her back into her cradle. 'Come,' she said to Rashid, and led him back to bed.

'It's strange,' he said, thinking in the dark, amazed at her wisdom. 'I feel like I know you, and yet I know nothing about you.'

She shrugged in his arms. 'There's not a lot to tell. I grew up in Sydney and became a child-care worker. And then, like I told you before, when my friend Sally and her husband opened the business, I joined Flight Nanny. End of story really.'

'What about family? Pets? Favourite colour?'

'Orange,' she said, with a smile. 'No pets. I'm away from home too much.'

'How did your parents die?'

'It was a glider crash, three years ago now. Dad was piloting when they collided with another glider and lost a wing. They were too close to the ground to have time to parachute out.'

He pulled her close, pressed his lips to her forehead. 'It must have been hard to lose them both together.'

'Yeah, and there are days when it's still hard. But overall, it gets easier with time. I was lucky enough to have them both until I was in my twenties. And I know it sounds a cliché, but it makes me feel better knowing they died doing something they both loved. Dad used to say you can never be freer than in the sky. I like to think of them soaring somewhere in the sky together.'

He squeezed her shoulders. 'Did you have any other family to help you, then?'

'I have a sprinkling of cousins but they're mostly all interstate so I hardly ever see them. Oh, except for one who lives in Sydney. But we're—well, we're not close.'

'Why's that?'

'Matt let me down badly over something.' Absently she ran her fingers through the coarse hair of his chest. 'I'm finished with him now. Sally's more family than any of them, really.'

'I'd be lost without my brothers, too. But then, they're not real brothers. Maybe that's what makes them special to us.'

'Maybe.' She squirmed and rolled over, as

if the topic made her too uncomfortable. 'You know, can we talk about something else?'

'I've got a better idea,' he said, liking the way her bottom wiggled so provocatively against him and feeling his body react accordingly. 'Maybe we should *do* something else.'

'Oh,' she said, when she caught on. 'I like the way you think.'

'And I like the way you do this…' He pulled her astride him and handed her a condom, liking, too, the way her eyes widened appreciatively as she realised how aroused he already was and took him in hand. He cupped one breast and ran a palm up her thigh while her fingers worked their magic on him as slowly she rolled the condom down his hard length. She gasped when his thumb grazed her inner lips.

'Oh, my,' she said, her job complete, but not her enjoyment as his fingers explored her slick folds. 'You do make it hard for a girl to concentrate on a task.'

'Maybe,' he said as he lifted her hips over him and positioned himself at her core, 'this might make it easier?'

And he pulled her all the long way down on him until he was seated deep inside her and she was stretched up like a cat, her back arched, all curves and sleekness above him such that he could not resist running his hand up over her smooth, firm flesh.

'Oh, yes,' she said on a sigh as her muscles let him go enough to lift herself from him until she was at his very tip, 'I think I can concentrate on this,' before she lost herself as she plunged down on him again.

'Stay here in Qajaran,' he said in between breaths as he brushed her hair from her face as they lay side by side waiting for their heart rates to return to normal. 'There is no need to go home yet.'

'Atiyah is settling,' she said, relishing the tickle of his fingers on her skin. 'She is becoming more used to Yousra and her new surroundings. Find her another carer and you will not need me soon.'

'I'm not asking you to stay for Atiyah's sake,' he said. 'I'm asking you for mine.'

And like one of the bursts of fireworks she'd witnessed against tonight's sky, hope bloomed bright and beautiful in her chest.

Could it mean that he was feeling something for her, as she felt for him? Was it possible that this crazy marriage could turn out to have a fairy-tale ending after all?

'I have my work…' she said, because a crazy idea still had to be met with a rational mind and she would be leaving Sally in the lurch at the worst possible time.

'I wouldn't expect you to drop everything and walk away empty-handed.'

'It's not about money.'

'No, but money can make problems easier to sort out,' he said, and she thought about the money that had got Sally and Steve to treatment in Germany.

'I guess that's true.'

'We'll work something out,' he said, kissing her brow.

'I haven't said I'll stay yet.'

'You haven't said you won't.'

Rashid left Tora in his bed with a smile on his face. It was perfect. She was perfect. When he'd agreed to come to Qajaran, doubt had been foremost in his mind. Need he do this, could he do this? And he'd decided to stay, and a lot of it was all down to Tora being here, right beside him all the way. When he'd been consumed by doubt, she'd been the one who'd convinced him he could be the leader Qajaran needed.

And the thought that she was leaving filled him with dread. He didn't want her gone. He wanted her to stay. More than that, when it all came down to it, he *needed* her to stay.

It was a strange feeling, this need. He'd never needed anyone in his life before, and if there was one thing his father's sudden and short-lived blip back into his life had reinforced in him, it was that he didn't need anyone else. That he was right to rely on his own devices and his desert brothers.

He knew for a fact his desert brothers would never betray him.

He'd never needed anybody else.

Until Tora.

His heart beat a little faster in his chest as he remembered how she'd looked when he'd left her. Sleep and sex tousled, her hair in wild disarray, and with a smile just for him, a smile that lit up his world.

He smiled to himself, even as he headed to work. Like the day of the ceremony, today had been declared a public holiday for everyone. Everyone, that was, who didn't happen to be the Emir or his Grand Vizier who both had work to do. He would make time later to see off Bahir and Kadar and their wives and children, who were heading off to Istanbul together. Zoltan would join him for some final talks this afternoon, before he and Aisha and the twins returned to Al-Jirad.

His thoughts returned to Tora and how he might get her to stay. The people would be happy, they clearly loved her as their sheikha, and so would his desert brothers and their wives. But he would be happier than all of them, because he wanted and needed her right there by his side.

His footsteps faltered on the marble tiles as a thunderbolt jagged through him.

Was this what his brothers always talked about, when they had found a woman to share their lives with? Was this what love felt like? Was Tora the one?

He shook his head, simultaneously baffled and in awe.

He'd never looked for love. He'd never expected to find it.

Still in a state of wonderment, he entered his office and found the unfaltering Kareem already there waiting for him.

'So, Kareem,' he said, feeling more light-hearted than he had in a long time, 'what do we have on the menu today?'

Kareem didn't seem to share his good mood. Instead he looked more troubled than Rashid had ever seen him, and older than his years, and for a moment Rashid wondered if the endurance test of the coronation had worn him out. 'Sire,' he said at length, 'I have news which may concern you.'

Rashid doubted it. Right now it would take a volcano to suddenly appear in the desert to concern him, and then only after it erupted. 'What is it?'

'A message was sent through the palace server.

I did not wish to bring it to your attention yesterday. It's from Sheikha Victoria to her cousin, a man called Matthew Burgess.'

Rashid remembered her talking about her cousins and how she didn't have anything to do with one in particular—he was sure that one was called Matthew.

'That doesn't sound right. Was it definitely her cousin?'

Kareem looked tense. 'A search proved it to be true.'

He told himself that it could still be innocent, that she might just have been informing him where to contact her, although why would Kareem consider that noteworthy?

'And do I really need to read a private email from Tora to her cousin?'

'I think perhaps you should.'

And a chill descended his spine as he took the letter from his vizier's hands.

Dear Matt

Don't think twice about the quarter of a million—it's a drop in the ocean to me right now. I'm just sorry you're having a tough time of it.

As it happens, I won't need to mortgage my home to help you out—we'll never have to mortgage anything ever again!—as I've stumbled on the mother lode: a rich petroleum billionaire who has royal connections. I know! The dollar signs in my eyes lit up too! I am confident I will be able to send you at least half a million dollars in one or two days.

Hang in there and keep watching that trust account—and keep listening for the ka-ching!

It's coming!

Your cousin

Victoria

PS Yes, blood really is thicker than water.

Rashid's blood ran so thick and cold it was practically curdling in his veins. A rich petroleum billionaire who has royal connections. The dollar signs in my eyes lit up too!

Something new and fragile threatened to crumble inside him then, his faith in her wanting to shatter into tiny pieces to scatter on the desert winds.

'You see, Excellency,' said Kareem, 'why I thought you might be interested in reading the contents.'

He could see all right, but no, this was Tora they were talking about. 'It cannot be true.' No way could it be true. This could not be Tora writing this. And even if it was… He flicked the paper in his hand. 'Surely this is some kind of joke?'

'I am sorry, sire, we thought the same, but there is more. It seems this Matthew Burgess and a solicitor colleague are both being investigated by the financial authorities for misappropriation of client funds.'

'There must be a misunderstanding, then. If this is the cousin Tora told me about, she doesn't have anything to do with him.'

Kareem bowed his head.

'What?' demanded Rashid.

'I wish I could say there had been some kind of mistake, but the solicitor's account at the heart of the fraud case—it is the same account the sheikha had us transfer the quarter of a million dollars to.' He paused. 'And there is evidence that the sheikha had repeated visits and phone calls to her cousin's office in Sydney before she came to Qajaran.'

'But she told me that she has nothing to do with the cousin who lives in Sydney. Is there another cousin?'

Kareem bowed again. 'I am sorry, sire. There is only the one.'

And Rashid's fragile new world splintered around him, leaving him shell-shocked and raw again, just as he'd been when he'd learned of his father's three-decade deception. But Tora's deception cut still deeper, because she'd played him for a fool.

'It's not about money,' she'd told him, after sending this message to her cousin.

It wasn't about money?

Liar.

'So her cousin is a crook,' said Rashid tightly. 'Which is no doubt why she needed the quarter of a million dollars so urgently, and another half million besides, so she could try to bail him out.'

'So it would seem, sire.'

And Rashid closed his eyes and turned his head to the ceiling. He had to hand it to her—all that talk that money couldn't fix things. All that holding out on him while all the time comforting him, reassuring him, making herself indispensable to him. All the while making out that she cared for Atiyah when it appeared now that all she had been concerned about had been riches.

His riches.

Betrayal wrapped its poisoned arms about him. There was a reason he didn't get close to anyone. There was a reason he preferred to wander this world alone.

'Kareem, as soon as the desert brothers and their wives have left today, I want you to remove Atiyah from Tora's suite and place a guard on her door. From then on until she leaves here, the sheikha is under house arrest.'

Kareem inclined his head. 'It will be done. I am sorry, sire.'

'Why are you sorry?'

'For pressing the urgency of your marriage to adopt Atiyah.'

'God, Kareem, it wasn't your fault I got lumbered with Tora. I chose her. I should have waited for you to find me a proper wife.'

'I did think, for a time, that she would make a good sheikha.'

Rashid ground his teeth together. He'd been thinking along the same lines. More fool him.

Tora took coffee and yoghurt with fruit on the terrace feeling happier than she'd felt for what seemed like ever. She ached in all kinds of places she hadn't known could ache and she didn't mind a bit because every twinge reminded her of why she ached and how she'd earned it, and every memory made her smile anew.

Because she'd spent a night making passionate love with Rashid.

Not sex. *Love.*

It was mad. She'd known Rashid for such a short time, but what she felt for him was special. Love? She didn't know, but she felt the bloom of warmth every time she thought of it. It was a new discovery, shiny and pretty and wondrous, and she wanted to take it out and examine it and hold it close to her heart.

Beside her on a rug under a sun shade Atiyah practised her push-ups, gurgling happily, and all of a sudden flipped herself over. She lay there on her back, looking totally surprised at her different view of the world.

'Oh, you clever girl,' Tora said, clapping her hands at this early milestone, and Atiyah broke into a gummy grin, suddenly delighted with herself.

And Tora couldn't wait to tell Rashid.

Surely this day could not get any more perfect?

CHAPTER FOURTEEN

THE WEATHER HAD turned humid and oppressive, the kind of day that made your clothes stick to your skin and made you want to stay in the cool inside the thick palace walls, and it was late afternoon before the two remaining women had a chance to venture outside to sit and drink tea by the pool in the courtyard before Aisha had to depart.

They had bade goodbye to Marina and Amber and their families earlier in the day and now Tora and Aisha sat in the shade, baby Atiyah lying sleeping in a cradle that Tora set swaying with a gentle push every little while, while Aisha's two-year-old twins ran around chasing each other. Jalil was bigger, and faster on his feet, but Kadija was more agile and would dart away at the last moment, shrieking in delight as her brother lunged for her and snatched only handfuls of air.

'Your children are beautiful,' Tora said, more than a little wistful that they would soon be gone. It had been hard for her to say goodbye to Marina and Amber, who had both hugged her and said they hoped to see her 'next time'. She hoped to see them again, too, but she couldn't afford to imagine herself a permanent place in Rashid's future on the strength of one night and a mere request to stay longer. No matter what this new-found emotion centred at her heart wove into wanting. It was all too new and there were too many unknowns, and what Rashid felt and wanted was the biggest unknown of them all.

Aisha beamed suddenly beside her, unable to suppress a smile. 'Thank you,' she said, putting her hand low over her belly and looking up at Tora with bright shining eyes as she reached across and squeezed Tora's hand with the other. 'I've been waiting to share the news with Zoltan ever since I had it confirmed today, but he and Rashid have been so busy. I told Marina and Amber just before they left, and I know we haven't known each other very long, but I'm bursting with the news and you feel like a friend already.' She took a breather. 'Jalil and Kadija are going to have a little brother or sister.'

'That's wonderful news,' Tora said. 'I'm so honoured that you'd tell me. Congratulations!'

'Thank you.' Aisha hugged her hands in her lap as she watched her twins. 'Zoltan will be so pleased. He thought after me getting pregnant so quickly with the twins that it would happen again just as easily.' Tora saw a glimmer of pain in her eyes and the words she hesitated over, the words she left unsaid. 'Of course, it wasn't that easy at all. But now…' and Aisha smiled again and looked radiant with it '…now he will be so thrilled.'

'You two are so much in love,' Tora said on a sigh. 'You deserve every happiness.'

Aisha nodded, adding a conspiratorial smile. 'Thank you, but, I have to admit, it didn't start out that way.'

'Really? You're both so perfect for each other, I imagined you two falling in love at first sight.'

Aisha laughed. 'That's very funny, given the first time we met I bit him on his hand, although, to be fair, he was wearing a mask so I couldn't see how handsome he was.' She seemed to think about that a second. 'No, actually that would have made no difference, because the second time we met I clawed his face with my nails, though that was after he told me we were to be married. Against my will, as it happened.'

'You were forced to marry Zoltan? That seriously happens?'

She nodded. 'Yes. It happens and I had no choice. I wanted to marry for love but my father said I had to marry Zoltan, or both our kingdoms would be compromised.'

'And so you went through with it.'

'I did. Zoltan wasn't happy though, when I refused to sleep with him on our wedding night.'

Tora was so shocked she laughed. 'You didn't?'

Aisha smiled and shrugged. 'How else could I show my displeasure at being forced into marriage? I did not know this man I was expected to fall into bed with. He was a stranger to me and I wanted a love match.'

'What happened?'

'He showed me he was a good man and I could not help but fall in love with him.'

Tora shook her head. 'Nobody would ever guess you two started out like that.'

'Don't think I'm the only one—Marina and Amber had no easy path to love either. You see, there is something you must understand about these four men, Zoltan and Bahir, Kadar and Rashid—they are like brothers, only their bond is stronger, and duty is everything to them. They may not like it, they may strain against their fate, but ultimately they know what they must do.

'But they are so focused on their duty they don't take easily to the concept of love. None of them had an easy upbringing, and they all grew up looking after themselves. They are so used to being in control of their lives and their destinies that love is foreign to them. They are caught unawares how powerful love can be, but when they do fall in love, they fall hard.

'It has been the same for Zoltan, Bahir and

most recently Kadar. And now Rashid is one hundred per cent focused on his new role and, in truth, is probably still coming to terms with this change in his life, but you will see, in time, Rashid will come good, too. He will be a good husband to you.'

And Aisha sounded so certain that Tora's uncertainties came brimming to the fore. 'Except this is still a marriage of convenience. As soon as we're divorced, he'll no doubt marry a meek Qajarese woman with the right connections the first chance he gets.'

Aisha shook her head. 'No, this cannot be true. I have seen you two together. I saw you during the coronation where Rashid's eyes followed your every move. We all saw him watching you. I cannot believe he would let you go, now that he's found you.'

Tora tried not to read too much into Aisha's predictions. 'He did ask me last night, to stay longer.'

Aisha smiled. 'You see! It is happening already. Soon he will not be able to imagine living without you. Do you love him?'

And Tora looked away to escape from the other woman's direct question and even more direct gaze. 'I… I'm not sure. How do you know for sure if you love somebody?'

Aisha put a hand over her heart. 'You feel it

here, and—' she touched her head '—you know it here and suddenly it consumes you and you need him with every fibre of your being. You know that without him, you can never be complete. And when you make love with the man you love, you are complete.'

Tora let go a breath she'd been holding.

Love.

That was how it had felt to her last night.

'So,' prompted Aisha. 'Is it love?'

'I think it is,' she said, smiling at the flutter in her heart as she admitted it. 'I think I've fallen in love with Rashid.'

'So here you all are.'

Tora spun around at Zoltan's voice, humiliated enough that he must have overheard her words, but no, it was worse than that, because there was Rashid, right beside him, and his eyes were as cold as the slabs of marble that lined the floor. She shivered from their impact as Zoltan leaned down and kissed his wife while the twins shrieked and came running to greet their father.

Tora looked away, busied herself looking anywhere but at Rashid and at those damning eyes.

Why would he be so angry, even if he'd overheard her? How could a few innocent words banish what they'd shared last night?

'Have you had a good day?' Zoltan asked, still

leaning over his wife, their faces mere inches apart. That was love right there, thought Tora. Love in abundance.

'The best,' Aisha replied, aiming a conspiratorial smile towards Tora. 'Just wait till I tell you.'

And a glance towards Rashid saw his eyes still locked on her, so cold and hard that she was almost sure she must have imagined last night in her dreams.

And if there was any love between her and Rashid, right now, it was one-sided. He stood in the terrace doorway looking as rigid and unmoving as if he'd been planted there and sent down roots.

'Our plane is ready,' Zoltan told his wife.

'Already we must go?' she said, smiling sadly in Tora's direction. 'It's been so good to be here. So good to meet you.' And she pulled Tora into a hug that felt bittersweet, because whatever her hopes and dreams, given the dark look on Rashid's face, she had an uneasy feeling in her stomach that she would never see Aisha or the other desert wives again.

Tora went to Atiyah's cradle, ready to take her inside, when Rashid suddenly stepped forward in her path. 'No. Leave her. I will take my sister.'

And Tora's gut clenched at the tone in his voice. Something was seriously wrong.

* * *

Aisha and Zoltan and the children were gone and Rashid must have spirited Atiyah off somewhere because she—along with Yousra—hadn't made an appearance since she'd returned to the suite.

But what had she done between this morning and this afternoon to deserve such a cold-shouldering? Other than to be overheard saying that she loved him?

Even if she hadn't intended blurting it out as she had, was that so serious a crime?

She sat down on the sofa and switched on her tablet. Maybe there would be some good news waiting for her, something to lighten this cloud of impending doom that she'd sensed in Rashid's cold eyes.

There was an email from her cousin she groaned at but ignored—no doubt Matt wondering where the money was—because there was one from Sally that demanded her attention—one that had the subject header Prayers needed!

Feeling sick to the stomach, she opened it up and read its contents as the cloud of impending doom circling above her head rained its poison down on her.

Oh, my God—please, God, no!

And the news was so awful, so devastating, that she had to tell someone, had to share this burden. She ran to her door and pulled it open, confused when she found two palace guards waiting outside, blocking her exit. She swept tears from her cheeks as she asked, 'What are you doing here?'

'By order of the Emir,' one proclaimed, 'you must remain where you are. You are now a prisoner of Qajaran.'

CHAPTER FIFTEEN

TORA STOOD IN the centre of her suite, too uptight to sit, too frozen by fear to move. There were guards on the terrace, too, and behind the interconnecting door to Rashid's suite. Guards everywhere, but why? On a day where it was sweltering outside, inside she felt chilled to the core.

Tora clutched at her goosebumped arms, her face still streaked with tears she'd shed in protest and shock at being arrested in a palace halfway around the world from her home.

A palace where nobody would ever find her, even if they knew where to come looking. And the vulnerability of her situation hit her. A lone woman, a long way from home, at the mercy of a man she'd thought she was beginning to understand—beginning to love.

Fool!

But what had she done to deserve being treated this way?

Nothing! She was sure of it.

She sniffed. She would make sure she told Rashid the same too.

A guard marched across the terrace in front of her windows. 'I want to see Rashid!' she called out.

The guard didn't so much as twitch in response, just kept right on marching as if she hadn't spoken.

'I *demand* to see the Emir!'

Tora waited, her heart thumping so loud in her chest, but nothing changed. Nobody was listening.

Nobody cared.

And her grief and pain and confusion coiled together inside her like the smoke from a candle flame that had been extinguished, acrid and swirling, until a new emotion rose out of it.

Fury.

It turned her shock to resolve and her tears to ice, setting her jaw to aching tight and her fingernails clawing into her arms. So the guard wouldn't tell Rashid she wanted to see him. So he wanted to make her wait. Well, let him. Because when he eventually arrived, she would be ready for him.

There was a thunder cloud hanging over him. Dark and threatening, it weighed heavily down upon him, blackening his world and poisoning his mood.

Tora.

He had not expected to be betrayed by her. Maybe at first he would have thought it possible. A woman picked up in a bar who coolly demanded a quarter of a million dollars when asked to name a price—why wouldn't he expect a woman like that to want to take advantage of the situation?

But that would have been at first.

Because since that time she'd worked her way into his life and under his skin. Floating on the air as she seemed to do in her silk robes, displaying an insight into economic and social matters he hadn't expected, telling him that he was strong.

And to top it all off, giving herself to him like a coronation gift, as if she were offering water to a man who'd been in the desert too long.

All the while it seemed she'd been scheming.

All the while waiting.

Well, now she could wait in her apartments. By the time he got to her, she would be a pathetic mess. She would apologise—profusely and with tears—and beg for his forgiveness, but there would be none. He would not fall for her ways again.

Why the hell was he waiting? He would tell her now. He stormed to his feet, upsetting a low table, and his anger went ballistic.

It was high time he told her.

* * *

Her door was flung open, and Tora held her breath. Rashid. At last!

He nodded to the guard who pulled the door shut, and then he looked grim-faced to where she stood in the middle of her room, her arms still crossed, her chin still high.

'What the hell is going on?' she demanded.

A dark eyebrow arched as he moved slowly towards her, and she could tell that if he had a shred of remorse for putting her in this situation, she couldn't see it anywhere in his stormy blue eyes. They were empty of anything but cold, hard resentment.

'Why, Sheikha, do you not like your new living arrangements? All this space to yourself, I see, and so much privacy. Who could ask for more? But if you have a complaint, there are stone cells in the floors below the palace, I believe, if these rooms are not to your satisfaction.'

Her chin ratcheted up a notch higher. 'Why am I prisoner here? What have I done?' Her voice broke on the last word and then her strength and resolve gave way. 'Rashid,' she appealed, taking a step closer even though the very air felt like bars between them. 'What is happening?'

He snorted. 'Didn't I tell you to be careful what you sent using the palace Internet? Didn't I warn you?'

He made no sense. She hadn't plastered anything up on social media. She hadn't sent anything she shouldn't.

'But then,' he continued, 'why would you listen to me? Blood *is* thicker than water, after all.'

'What?'

'Oh, come now, Sheikha, surely you can't have forgotten this little gem? *"The dollar signs in my eyes lit up too!"* Or maybe this one will strike a chord: *"keep listening for the ka-ching"*.'

And like a sledgehammer it hit her. The email she'd sent to Matt. The nonsense email to get him excited and frothing at the mouth with anticipation.

'You read my emails? How dare you? That was private.'

'What did you think I meant when I warned you? Of course the palace has to monitor communication coming in and out. Did you think your little missive to your cousin would go unnoticed—a cousin you are supposedly finished with now?'

'I *am* finished with him.'

'What, after you sent him the two hundred and fifty thousand dollars, or will that be after the five hundred thousand you have promised him next?'

'What? I didn't send that money to Matt—it went to a solicitor who—' And with a sickening thud, she realised just who she'd sent the funds through—the very solicitor Matt had instructed to draw up the documents complete with the small print she'd been too naive to read and so signed her inheritance over to him. And if Matt was in some kind of financial trouble, then, chances were…

'Let me finish your sentence.' Rashid confirmed it for her. 'It went to a solicitor who is now being investigated, along with your beloved cousin, for misappropriation of funds.'

Tora squeezed her eyes shut, reeling at her naivety, cursing the rush she'd been in that she'd trusted a colleague of Matt's. What if that money, too, had been lost?

But surely Rashid couldn't believe that she'd sent the money to Matt. 'I didn't know about the charges. I didn't know any of that. Matt gave me his solicitor's name because he was dealing with my parents' estate. But the money wasn't for him. That went—'

'Then why did you tell him not to worry about it?'

'No. Listen,' she said, putting out her hands in supplication, 'you're confusing two different things. Matt cheated me out of my inheritance from my parents' estate—that was the two hundred and fifty thousand he was talking about. When he asked for more, I thought I'd send him a taste of his own medicine. What I sent him was rubbish, Rashid, to lure him in and make him think I'd stumbled on a fortune and was going to share it with him. You have to believe me.'

'Two hundred and fifty thousand dollars,' Rashid said, ignoring her explanation, 'which just *happens* to be the same amount of money you asked for and got.'

'Yes, because I had promised it elsewhere and I needed it as quickly as possible.'

'Why? What was so urgent that you were so desperate to get the money then?'

'Because Sally's husband has cancer and they needed the funds to get him to a cancer clinic in Germany. And I'd promised to loan them the money from my inheritance because they'd already mortgaged their house and they'd exhausted every other means. That's where your precious two hundred and fifty thousand dollars went, and Steve's there now lying in that clinic, fighting for his life and close to death and now it looks like everything I've done has been for nothing.'

Her vision blurred and swam and she dropped her face to the floor. She didn't know when she'd started crying, she hadn't been aware of the tears falling, but now there was no stopping the torrent coursing down her face. Because if Steve died, everything would have been for nothing.

The sound of a clap forced her head up. Followed by another. A slow clap coming from Rashid that matched the slow pace of his feet as he drew closer to where she had fallen. 'Bravo, Ms Burgess, that was an award-winning performance. It had pathos, melodrama, even tears. Unfortunately some of us recognise that was all it was—an act. I didn't see you looking too upset last night when you were coming apart in my bed. I didn't see any tears fall then.'

She sniffed. 'Sally wrote this morning with the news.'

'Oh, this morning. How convenient.'

'Steve is dying. It's the truth!'

'I don't think you'd recognise the truth if it slapped you in the face. You climbed aboard that royal jet and ever since then you've been scheming to make it worthwhile to you and your crooked cousin. You played it well. Exceptionally well. One time a siren, another a virgin Madonna, you kept ducking and weaving and spinning your web of lies so well that you almost had me convinced that you were special, that there might even be a future for us beyond this short-term deal.'

His lip curled. 'What a fool I've been.' His cold dark eyes were filled with abhorrence as they raked over her, all but scraping her skin with their intensity. 'And I must be a fool because

I thought—I actually thought…' He shook his head. 'A fool. You will stay here in your rooms until it is time to send you home.'

'Rashid,' she begged as he turned to leave, because in his words was a tiny kernel, a glimmer of hope, if she could only prove to him that she was telling the truth. 'Please, I beg of you…'

His feet paused at the door. 'What?'

'There is one thing you should know. One thing you have to believe.'

'Well?'

She licked her lips, her heartbeat frantic as she prepared to lay it on the line and bare herself to him utterly. 'I couldn't do the things you say. I would never betray you. Because… Because, I love you.'

He laughed, the sound cold and jagged as it echoed around her room, until she felt as if her heart had been sliced apart. 'Nice try.'

And then he was gone.

She threw herself down onto her bed and let herself weep in great heaving sobs—because she'd only ever married Rashid to secure the funds for Steve's treatment and, somewhere along the line, she'd fallen in love with a despot in the process, a despot who'd laughed at her when she'd bared her soul to him.

And now Steve was fighting for his life in a German clinic and it had all been so pointless.

It had all been for nothing.

And she hated the man who had done this to her with all her heart.

The man she'd thought she had loved.

She loved him. Talk about desperate. As if he'd believe that. As if she'd thought it would excuse what she'd done.

Atiyah was crying when he returned to his rooms and the black cloud above his head thundered and roared.

'She won't stop,' a tearful Yousra said. 'She wants Tora.'

'Give her to me!' he demanded, and the young woman's eyes opened wide with surprise, but still she handed the bundle over. He juggled the unfamiliar weight, the arms and legs working like little pistons, the face screwed up and red, and he caught a flailing arm with one finger and tucked her in close to his chest as he tried to remember how Tora had told him to try to calm her. 'Atiyah,' he said, trying to stop the storm cloud hanging over him from making him shout over her screams, 'Calm down. Calm down.'

He walked with her one way, he walked back the other, but there was no settling her. 'Atiyah,' he said, 'little sister, you must stop this.' And on impulse, when he could not think of anything else that might help, he started humming the tune, the lullaby he'd heard Tora sing to her, the lullaby that had been dredged up from the depths of his memories. And eventually, somewhere along the line, the notes filtered through to the tiny infant and Atiyah's cries became more brief, staccato bursts between the listening moments, bursts that became hiccups. Until finally she fell silent apart from a low whimpering sound.

'Is she asleep?' Yousra whispered in awe. And he shook his head as he sang that soft lullaby, because, while her face had unscrunched, she was wide awake and staring up at him, a frown knitting her brow as she focused intently on his face, almost as if she recognised him.

He stared back at her, equally fascinated until he came to the end of the song and he smiled, and the little girl wiggled in his arms and smiled right back.

And his world turned on its axis and he knew it would never be the same.

'Like the world lights up and wraps you in love.' Tora had said that.

And yet he should have known that, because that was exactly how he'd felt when Tora had smiled at him. When she'd come apart in his arms. When he'd seen tears in her proud eyes at his coronation.

Those tears… Had she been scheming even then? How could she have known he'd turn to her in that moment? How could she have faked those tears? Tora had been the one who had got him through the coronation. Knowing she was there had been his one constant. Having her in his corner had lent him strength and made him wonder if their relationship could not be more permanent.

She'd made his duty more possible, more bearable, more palatable.

She'd made him wish she could stay by his side for ever.

She'd said she'd never betray him.

She'd said she loved him.

Oh, God, and arresting her was how he repaid her? He'd been so angry, had felt so betrayed, so manipulated, as if he'd been played for a fool from the start.

And the rank, horrible feeling in his gut told him that they had got things very wrong, and that he'd been the fool all along, he hadn't needed anyone to play him.

He had to find the truth—find the story behind the email to her cousin—there had to be proof. He owed her that much. There was an email this morning, she'd said, saying her friend was dying. It would be easy enough to check. Surely there would be something to prove or disprove her story one way or another. 'Yousra,' he said, the child still held close in his arms. 'Get me Kareem.'

* * *

An hour later, he had what he needed. A small stack of printed emails. 'Innocuous,' Kareem had labelled them. 'There was no mention of any amount of money.'

And Rashid believed him. Innocuous by themselves, but together with her story they painted a different picture... You're a lifesaver... Next stop, Germany! And the kick to the heart he deserved with the subject header on the email that had come overnight—Prayers needed!—and he knew with an icy cold rush down his spine that she'd been telling the truth.

And he dropped his head into his hands.

What the hell had he done?

And how was he ever to make amends?

CHAPTER SIXTEEN

TORA'S HEAD JERKED up from her pillow when she heard the sound of the door opening. For a moment she hoped it was Rashid so she could tell him exactly what she thought of him. She got out of bed and ran her fingers over her cheeks. Her tears had dried in the heat of her growing anger, but her skin felt tight, as if it were crusted with salt.

But it wasn't Rashid returning, but two young women, smiling shyly and holding baskets. They bid her to sit down and fed her honey tea while they brought out warm towels to wash her face and hands, and a hairbrush to brush her hair. There was even a freshly laundered gown to wear, and Tora didn't know what it meant but it was so blissful to clean the salt from her skin that she went along with it.

'Come with me, Sheikha Victoria,' the guard said, when she was feeling refreshed and human again and the women had vanished.

'What's going on?' she asked. 'Where are you taking me?' But he said nothing, just turned and led the way out.

Only one guard, she thought as she followed him. There had been four outside her doors and now only one—what did that mean?

'Where is the Emir?' she asked, but the man in front of her said nothing as he strode ahead of her through the long corridors and past the accumulated treasures of millennia and out the front doors of the palace and into an inky night.

A car idled quietly, its lights on low beam.

And there was Kareem, standing there, watching her approach. He bowed low, his hand on his chest.

'Sheikha,' he said. 'I have done you a great disservice. Please forgive me.'

And she guessed it was Kareem who had been alerted to her email to Matt and who had then alerted Rashid.

'It doesn't matter, Kareem. It was never meant to be. Can you tell me what is happening?'

'You are leaving,' he said, and, as if to support his words, her suitcase was delivered to the top of the steps. She swallowed.

'Now?' she said, caught between relief and a pang of regret for all she'd leave behind. The soft velvet night sky. Atiyah. Her heart. 'Already?'

'Already. His Excellency insisted.'

'Where is Rashid?'

'Waiting at the plane. He thought you would be happier travelling to the airport without him.'

Coward, she thought, but it was an accusation tinged with sadness. So she was to be seen off the premises like an employee who had been dismissed, her possessions hastily flung together, no chance to say goodbye to those she wished to? There was a lump in her throat the size and shape of a small child. 'You'll give Atiyah a hug for me?' she said, trying to push back on the sting of tears, and Kareem solemnly nodded.

She hauled in a breath, casting a look over her shoulder at the amazing fairy-tale palace that wasn't, before she turned back to Kareem and said with false brightness, 'Then let's go.'

He saw the headlights approach from where he stood at the foot of the stairs and felt sick to the stomach. She was leaving. Well, she'd always been going to leave, she was just leaving a little earlier, that was all.

And how could he not let her go? How could he keep her here as his prisoner and punish her for his own blind stupidity? How could he expect her to forgive him?

The car drew alongside the plane, its engines starting to whine, pulling up so the back door lined up with the red carpet that had been rolled out waiting for it, and Kareem emerged and offered his hand to the other passenger. Rashid swallowed.

Tora.

Looking like a goddess. Wearing the robe of orange and yellow she'd worn that day when they'd toured Malik's palaces. Such a few days ago and yet it seemed like a lifetime, so much had happened, so much had been felt. He saw her thank Kareem as he handed her out and retrieved her suitcase and then she glanced up and her eyes snagged on his. She looked away at her feet, and his heart snapped in two.

Well, what did he expect? It was no more than he deserved. She'd told him she loved him and he'd flung that love back in her face with a few choice insults besides. Call himself an Emir? A ruler of men? He couldn't even rule his own heart and mind. And if he couldn't make them act in consensus, how was he supposed to manage a country?

As he might have, with this woman by his side. He might have believed it was possible.

'Tora,' he said as she drew closer.

She angled her head, her eyes sharp like daggers, even if their edges seemed a little dulled with disappointment. 'Seeing me off the premises, Rashid? Making sure I don't escape with the silverware.' She held her arms out. 'Do you need to frisk me to make sure I haven't run off with any of Qajaran's treasures to pawn when I get home?'

He sucked in air that smelt of aviation fuel. He

deserved that. 'I was wrong,' he said. 'And in so many ways, and I know I can never apologise for all the wrongs I have done to you. But please believe me when I say I am truly sorry for the hurt I have done to you.'

Her lips pressed tightly together. 'Well, I guess that's all right, then. So, what about my divorce?'

'You will be notified when it is finalised.'

He saw her hesitate. 'What will become of Atiyah now?'

And it struck him that even in the midst of her own private hell, she was worried about his sister. His sister, for whom Tora had cared more and been more loving. God, he'd been a fool!

'She will be fine. She smiled at me tonight.'

'She did?' And Tora smiled, too, for a moment, until she remembered why she was here. 'Excellent,' she said before her teeth found her lip, and she looked up at the stairs, putting one hand on the rail. 'I'm looking forward to being back in Sydney.'

'Tora,' he said, stopping her from taking that first step just yet, 'once upon a time, you said you loved me. Did you mean it?'

She turned her head to the velvet sky and the wide belt of stars that was more clearly visible now they were out of the city precinct. 'I thought I did. And then I was just so angry with you, that it blocked everything out. I hated you for what you had done and what you had believed of me. After everything we had been through. I was so angry.'

He closed his eyes. 'And now?'

'Now I'm just sad for what could have been.'

And he couldn't let her go without telling her. 'I know it's too late, but I am a fool where love is concerned, but I want you to know that there was love between us. There is love that I feel for you.'

She swallowed back on a sob. So good of him to tell her that now, when he was putting her on a plane to leave. 'Do you call it love to judge someone as guilty before you even ask them for the truth? Do you call it love to treat that person like a criminal? Because if you do, you have a very warped idea of love.'

'Tora, I am so sorry. I didn't want to believe it was true, but you said you had nothing to do with your cousin, and there was evidence you'd spoken to him just recently, and I felt betrayed and deceived and it was like my father all over again, except this time it was you, and that felt a hundred times worse.'

She stared at him. 'My darling cousin stole my inheritance. All the money from my parents' estate. All the money I'd promised Sally and Steve. I'd just come from a meeting with him to tell me the happy news that all the money was gone. Why do you think I was so angry that night in the bar?'

He hung his head. 'God, I'm a fool. I will never make up to you the wrongs I have done you.'

'No,' she said. 'I don't believe you will. Goodbye, Rashid.' And she turned and fled up the stairs into the plane, knowing she had to get into the safety of the cabin before she lost it completely. Knowing she had to escape while she had the chance, while she still had one last shred of dignity intact, even if her heart lay broken into tiny pieces.

Something was wrong. Tora blinked into wakefulness after a tortured sleep. 'We're coming in to land,' the flight attendant said.

'Already?' said Tora, knowing she couldn't possibly have slept for that long.

'Yes,' said the attendant, clearing away cups and plates. 'If you look outside your window, you'll see the lights of Cologne ahead.'

Cologne?

'We're landing in Germany?'

'But of course,' said the attendant. 'Didn't you know?'

Sally hugged her friend so tight when Tora reached the hospital that she thought she might snap in two but she didn't mind one little bit. 'I couldn't believe it when I heard you were coming. And now you're here!' And she hugged her again.

'How's Steve?' Tora asked, hoping above hope that Sally's happiness wasn't solely down to her arrival.

Sally smiled over clenched teeth, a tentative smile of optimism. 'We thought it was the end—it looked like the end—and the doctors suggested trying something experimental but it was so expensive and I couldn't give them the go ahead, but then some anonymous benefactor contacted the clinic just last night and asked them to pull out all stops.' She shook her head. 'You wouldn't believe the difference in him in just a few hours. It's a miracle,' she said, and fell into her friend's arms again.

Anonymous benefactor?

Tora had a clue she knew exactly who it was and why he'd done it. And a broken heart made its first tentative steps to heal and love again.

She was punch drunk when she wrote the email. High on life and one life in particular, who was looking more human every day as he made a steady recovery. High on the happiness that her friend radiated constantly.

She hit Send and turned off her tablet and sat back on the lounge chair of the tiny flat she shared with Sally, feeling the rapid beating of her heart.

Well, it was out there. Now all she could do was wait.

CHAPTER SEVENTEEN

THERE WAS A glow coming from the courtyard, coming from inside the Pavilion of Mahabbah. And when a smiling Kareem led her inside, she could see why. The pavilion was lit with a thousand candles, their flames flickering and dancing in the night breeze, and for a moment as Kareem disappeared there was just the croak and plop of frogs amongst the lily pads and the haunting cries of the peacocks as she took it all in.

And then there were footsteps, and he was standing there in the doorway, Rashid—her Rashid—his dark features and golden skin standing out in his snowy white robes. So handsome. So darkly beautiful.

'Tora,' he said, blinking as if she were some kind of vision. 'But how—?'

'Kareem helped me.'

'But you came back,' he said, as if he couldn't believe it, his eyes full of wonder as his eyes drank her in.

'How could I not come back?'

'But after everything I did, after all the wrongs I did you.'

'You did some right. You helped Sally and Steve when they had nowhere else to turn to. You did a good thing. Steve's doing well. It's a miracle and we all have you to thank.'

'What else could I do? I had to do something.'

'It was a good thing you did. A generous thing. Thank you.'

'Thank you for coming to tell me that.' He gave a small sigh, a brief smile. He was a man at a loss. 'Did you want to see Atiyah? She's sleeping now, but you can stay a little while?'

'I'd love to see her.'

'That's good.' He looked around as if for Kareem, frowning as he seemed to notice for the first time the candles and the decorations. 'I imagine Kareem's organised a suite for you?'

'Rashid.'

'What?'

'There's another reason I came.'

His eyes grew wide. 'What?'

'When I left here, I wanted to hate you. You made that harder with what you did for Sally and Steve—'

'That doesn't make up for what I did.'

'I know. But while I sat there supporting Sally, I had time to think. And I thought about all the time that I watched you struggle with responsibilities that had been thrust upon you, struggle with the demands and needs of a tiny child you'd never asked for from a father who'd cast you into the world alone, even if to protect you—I thought about all that time, and how I could see you were a good man.'

'I was not good to you.'

'Not then, it's true, but what man would act differently when he'd been subject to the turmoil of your life, when he'd felt betrayed by the most important of people, his own father? How could he trust anyone ever again?'

'I should have trusted you.'

She put a finger to his lips to silence him. 'What's done is done. Can't we draw a line under what happened in the past? Can't we start anew?'

She saw hope swirling in the deep blue depths of his eyes. 'What are you saying?'

'I'm saying that, once upon a time, you hinted that you loved me, at least a little. I'm asking if you still do, and if you would do me the honour of marrying me, for real this time.'

'Marry you?'

'Yes. Because I love you, Rashid, for better or for worse. But I hope it's for ever.'

'Yes!' he cried as he picked her up in his arms and spun her around. 'A thousand times yes. I love you so much, Tora,' Rashid said, his lips hovering over hers. 'You have turned my life from a desert into an oasis. You have given life where there should be none. I owe you everything. And I will love you to my dying day.'

Tora smiled beneath his lips. 'As I will love you, Rashid. Aisha told me you desert brothers don't fall easily, but you fall hard.'

'I never expected to fall in love. I didn't think it was possible. But now I can't imagine a day in my life without you being in it.'

'That's good,' she said, 'because I don't plan on going anywhere without you.'

'You'll never have to, ever again.'

And they made love there that night, in the Pavilion of Mahabbah, the pavilion of love, the first night in all their nights of for ever.

EPILOGUE

THEY WERE MARRIED for the second time in front of the iconic sails of the Sydney Opera House alongside the sparkling waters of the harbour on which pleasure craft made the most of a perfect sunny day. Overlooking it all sat the magnificent backdrop of the Sydney Harbour Bridge.

The bridal procession was strikingly original, a confection of sheer joy, and headed by the combined children of the desert brothers and their wives strewing rose petals and jasmine flowers, the older children holding the hands of the younger ones and guiding them back to the red carpet when they strayed off course or got distracted, to the delight of all the assembled. Behind them came the three stunning matrons of honour wearing gowns in glorious jewel colours, ruby, emerald and sapphire, the Sheikha Aisha and Princess Marina and the blonde, blue-eyed Amber.

And last came Tora, wearing a sleeveless gown of golden silk ruched over her breasts and hips with a sweeping train and with her hair piled high and studded with champagne-coloured pearls and who was walked along the foreshore to meet her groom by the three best men, Zoltan, Bahir and Kadar.

At the very front stood Rashid, waiting as each group made its way to him, waiting impatiently for the moment he would be joined by his glowing bride. Under Qajarese law, he had been a married man for six months, and Tora a married woman. Six months during which the state of Qajaran had grown up, a period full of the necessary aches and pains of change but the benefits were already there, the confidence of the economy picking up, the lacklustre tourism sector finally getting off the ground.

Six months during which he had grown up and changed and become the ruler Qajaran needed, but only, he knew, because this woman had been by his side every step of the way.

Half a year they had been together, but today was the start of their real marriage, he knew. Today what had begun as a hastily arranged marriage of convenience would become a marriage of necessity, a marriage of free choice, a marriage to last until the end of days.

He smiled at the children as they made their way closer, saw Yousra in the throng holding a growing Atiyah in her frothy white dress, a white ribbon tying up her black curls, and he knew life was good.

The three brides of his brothers, their beautiful faces beaming, stepped to his left. How was it possible for his brothers to find such remarkable women, each and every one of them, and yet to leave the pearl of the collection for him? How lucky was he?

She was drawing closer, his brothers cutting in on each other to take turns on her arms. She was laughing at something one of them said and Rashid was struck by her beauty and her joy. She was radiant. She looked up then, and the laughter died on her lips as their eyes locked. He saw the cognac-coloured eyes darken with smouldering need and the smile that she gave just to him and his heart swelled.

And then she was there before him and his three desert brothers lifted her hand to place in his, before, with a slap to his back, they peeled away to stand on his right.

'You look beautiful,' he said softly. 'I love you.'

'As I love you,' she said, unable to stop the two tears of joy that squeezed unbidden from her eyes. 'For ever.'

It was a fairy tale, it occurred to Tora in that moment as she looked up into the dark gaze of the man she loved. A tale of trials and tribulations decorated with palaces and pavilions, peacocks and fountains. A tale of the exotic. And yet a tale of the most basic human needs.

Like life.

She glanced towards her friend Sally where she sat beaming alongside Steve in his wheelchair—Steve, who was growing stronger by the day. Sally blew her a kiss and Tora smiled back, before looking up to the sky and feeling her mother and father soaring in the heights and beaming down upon her on her proudest day. They were here, she knew, and it was good.

Even better when she felt Rashid's lips on her cheek. 'You have made me the happiest man in the world,' he whispered, and she wondered just how much joy it was possible to feel before one exploded with it.

For together they had conquered the tests put before them, had overcome their own fears and confronted their own feelings, and as their reward they had won the greatest prize of all. Had earned the greatest gift of all, for even life itself was worthless without it.

Love.

'Dearly beloved,' the celebrant began then as the gulls wheeled in the sky above and the passing ferry drivers tooted their horns in celebration, 'we are gathered here today for this very special Christmas wedding…'

* * * * *